Loving a Selfie

BEATRICE FISHBACK

No part of this book may be reproduced in any form or by any electronic or mechanical means, including information storage and retrieval systems, without written permission from the author, except for the use of brief quotations in a book review.

Copyright © 2016 by Beatrice Fishback
ISBN-10 : 1549890557
ISBN-13 : 978-1549890550
All rights reserved.

Acknowledgments

Thanks to the best critique partners in the world: Irene Onorato, Linda Robinson, and Dana K. Ray.

To my God. Every word comes from you and I give you thanks for the gift of words.

Jim. The man who makes my world complete.

Loving a Selfie

Chapter One

I'M NEVER GOING to let anything hurt me again.

Like the mantra from a script, Shelley mentally repeated the words as she stepped from the shower, dried her hair, and slipped into a simple charcoal-grey dress.

A swift brush through her hair, swipe of bright pink lipstick across firm lips and she was ready to conquer the world. Shelley pressed her mouth tightly into a tissue and tossed it into the small trashcan.

After a quick overview in the mirror, she twisted away from the reflection, and her long hair swished across her shoulders and neck. Shelley hit the *off* button on the HDTV remote and the news channel faded from view.

She left the bedroom, forced a confident smile, trounced down the steps, and grabbed her peacoat from the front hall closet. Her agenda included a quick stop at the coffee shop for a daily latte with soy, an annoying delay at the doctor's office for a test he'd insisted she take, and then on to work. As if on cue, December's brilliant sunshine and bitter air hit her straight on as she stepped out.

The sun's glow formed a halo around her frame and

announced to the world she was alive and well, honoring it with her presence. Shelley had been dubbed Baby Barbie as a five-year-old. Now called 'hard as Shell' by her peers, she was extremely proud of this latest title.

"Ladies and gentlemen, please welcome Miss Shelley Auburn." Freddie Sloan, co-worker and weak link in the office staff chain as far as Shelley was concerned, gave her the platform and sat on a nearby chair.

"Thank you, Freddie." She wrinkled her nose at him like he smelled of sour cabbage, then caught herself and smiled with the practiced coy of a sweet teen. "You've been such a help organizing this meeting."

Freddie beamed like a pup rewarded with a treat. If he had a tail, she was sure he'd wag his bottom with gleeful energy. Instead, he lowered his head and waved with the gesture of deference to a queen.

She turned to the audience. "Thank you for being a part of this important and wonderful day in the expansion of Universal Station. U.S. is indicative of what we stand for. It is all about us. We are here to conquer the unconquerable. We like to think of ourselves as disruptive innovation. Before long, everyone will be looking here for their answers, to U.S. for guidance and for U.S. to take care of every aspect of their lives."

Forceful applause stirred her self-awareness with the power of a stoked steam engine and temporarily swept away the hurting throb that lived within her like an unwelcome roommate. She patted her palms downward, and the crowd slowly eased their clapping. Truth be told, Shelley loved the adulation and would've allowed the noise to continue until their hands fell off—an aphrodisiac to her ego.

"Once the final pieces are put into place, we will infiltrate social media with the punch of an earthquake that will rock the world. In taking over Google, Bing, and every other prehistoric archive and combining their capabilities into one, we will have total dominance. All that's left is to tweak a few bugs in the system. This, however, requires a little more time and greater investment. That's where you, our friends and co-laborers in this endeavor, come into play. We can't achieve our final push without your empowerment, which includes financial assistance. We as a company want to thank you for considering additional revenues to fulfill this dream."

Shelley stepped away from the podium and allowed the mostly male audience to have a view of her twenty-nine-year-old, nearly perfect physique. It gave the desired effect. Those in the front row gazed at her as if Angelina Jolie had arrived. She knew the looks and took advantage of them, lowered then raised her eyelids, and gave a farewell wave.

She walked off the platform and into the backstage, clapping quietly with positive self-appraisal. Although using her female wiles was demeaning, there was something to be said about using her advantages over others.

"Well done, Shell." Marjorie Malloy, CEO of U.S., grabbed her arm. "You had them eating out of your hand. I knew you'd be the right leverage to incite further financial gain." Marjorie's smile did nothing to alleviate the fact that her face sagged with the semblance of a long-faced hound dog.

"Never a problem."

"Before long this company will be your total responsibility."

Shelley smiled the "I've just eaten the sweetest candied apple" look. "The crowd was putty. Now they're all yours, Missus Malloy."

Marjorie walked out onto the stage and Shelley disappeared

into the massive office building that housed the largest social site ever established.

Shelley took the enclosed blue-glassed elevator to the second level, stepped out, and overlooked the sea of workers. Universal Station was a dream launched by Marjorie and her now deceased husband, Jordan.

Swags of Christmas greenery, tiny tea lights and an oversized Christmas tree dominating one corner created holiday ambience.

Young, vibrant students clicked away at terminals and inserted data in the latest computerized boards that hummed the sound of a thousand bees. Their pay was minimum, their hours long, yet they too were enticed with Universal Station's possibilities. Unfortunately, they would never see an iota of the billions the site would eventually procure.

She opened up her arms wide. "Ah, this is all I've ever dreamed of. Being prepped to take over U.S. will be the first step to my next ambition."

"And what would that be?" John Cox came near and gazed at her with laser penetration. "I mean your next ambition?" The curved turn of his lip and deepening dimple clearly displayed his tease.

She slapped his arm and felt the muscle flex beneath. "How dare you listen in to my musings without being asked?" Something about him disarmed her every time. It wasn't those large brown eyes that begged a girl to get lost in them. It wasn't even his over six-foot frame and slightly curly black hair that was forever falling over his brows asking to be put back into place. It was something else entirely that she couldn't quite put her finger on.

No one ever got the better of Shelley, but John made her behavior of a three-year-old wanting attention rear its ugly head and the unwanted roommate of pain to rise to the surface. She shoved the pain into its proper place, a habit she'd practiced and perfected over many years.

"Were you stalking me?" She teased, batting her eyelashes in hopes of breaking his defenses.

"You know better."

"Yes. Unfortunately, I do." She drew closer and clutched his arm with her nails.

He backed away.

"Why, John, I do believe you're afraid of me."

"Afraid?" A blush burst from his neck, up his face, across his ears, and along his temples. "What do I have to be afraid of?"

Shelley stepped toward him, nearly touched his chin with her nose and spoke with a sultry whisper, "Most men would move nearer me. You pull back every time I get close." She lifted one leg in a flamingo stance.

"You're right."

Shelley lowered her leg and stepped back. "I am?"

"Any man would love to be close to you."

"So?" She moved back in his direction.

"So. I'm not any man that you'd be interested in, so why waste our time?"

Shelley rubbed his arm with the stroke of a purring kitten. "Why would you think it would be a waste of time?"

"Because you want this." He waved his hand to the masses below.

"Don't you? Be honest. Doesn't standing here evoke a sense of strength and sheer power as if you could conquer the world?"

"I have no interest in conquering the world."

"Oh, that's right. As Universal's spiritual director you're compelled to let everyone know about God. That *He's* the ruler of this world. Isn't that it?" Shelley stepped away from him and leaned on the railing. "You can have your God, John. This is my god, right here." She waved to one of the students who had looked up and smiled.

"Shelley, you didn't answer my question."

"What's that?" She turned back.

"What *is* your next ambition? Will what you achieve next ever be enough to make you happy?"

The seriousness of his tone and the ache of tenderness in his eyes took Shelley by surprise. "Why John Cox, I do believe you care for me after all."

"I care only that you're right with God. All of this will pass away, and then what will you have?"

"Money?" Her tinkled laugh mocked his sincerity.

"Never mind." He walked toward the elevator.

"John?"

"Yes." He pushed the button and the glass doors opened.

"Thanks." She turned serious for a brief moment.

"For what?"

"For being you."

John stepped into the elevator and the doors closed. Shelley watched as the glassed box lowered. She returned her attention to the teeming workers. "I'm glad you've got God, John. But I want oh so much more."

Shelley rubbed the cool railing and gazed across the lower level to the other side. Patrick Malloy, son and heir of Marjorie and Jordan's fortune, waved.

"Now there's my next ambition." She blew him a kiss.

Patrick reached his hand out as if to grab her floating sign of affection and smiled. His dumpy cheeks attested to tastes of the finer things in life. Shelley determined to share every single fine thing he owned.

Chapter Two

JOHN WANDERED INTO his office and closed the door.

A gold nameplate, etched with *John Cox, Spiritual Advisor*, sat on the edge of the mahogany-topped desk.

Nothing but the best, for the best man I know. Jordan Malloy had bragged to John the first time he'd given a grand tour of the suite. Anyone in their right mind would envy the lap of luxury he had the privilege of entering each day.

The room, big enough to hold two Chesterfield sofas that faced each other, an antique Chippendale coffee table between them, and two silver candelabras as centerpieces, offered an intimate setting for those wishing counsel. Every piece of furniture had been handpicked and shipped from *Chapel Street Furnishings of London*.

Some days, his office reminded him of a judge's chambers. The twenty-foot ceiling of glass windows revealed a view of D.C. a lawyer would die for. Other days, it felt like a tomb.

He walked past the desk, stood near the window and gave a long sigh that, had it enough power, would have blown out one of the panes.

"How I miss you, Jordan." He spoke to his watery reflection

as clouds pregnant with moisture had rolled in. The rain streamed along the glass with a waterfall effect and melted the last remaining snow mounds dotting the ground below. "When you asked me to take this position, you said you wanted a spiritual influence for your employees." With Jordan now gone, John knew he had become a figurehead with no real authority, and even less opportunity to offer his services.

Marjorie had kept him on the payroll for her dead husband's benefit and as a political statement. Nothing more.

"What am I doing here? No one comes to me for help." John heaved another sigh and walked to the bookshelf. "I'm useless."

He ran his index finger along the bindings. Every book he'd ever dreamed of owning lined the shelves. He pulled one out. A first-print, leather-bound copy of *A Tale of Two Cities*.

Rap. Rap. Rap. He jumped. "Who's there?" John rushed to the door and coughed to cover up his surprise at the visitor.

Patrick Malloy, easily six inches shorter than John, shuffled his feet and kept his eyes lowered. "Do you have a minute?"

"Um. Sure. Please come in."

"Not used to having folks stop by unexpectedly, I gather?" Patrick assessed the room with his large, blue eyes set in doughy flesh.

"You could say that."

"Father was so pleased to have you here."

"Things have changed somewhat since he's been gone, though. So what can I do for you, Mister Malloy?"

"Call me Patrick. Please." He waddled to one of the settees, sat and propped his feet on the ten thousand dollar table. "Do you have anything to drink? Say a Perrier?"

"Of course." John served Patrick a crystal glass with a few ice cubes and sparkling water and sat across from him. "Now what can I do for you?"

"You can give me some advice."

"That's what I'm here for." He sat back, rested his right foot across his left knee and draped his arm across the back of the sofa. *Relax. Just relax. He's only here to ask advice, not fire you.*

"It's Shelley."

"Ah." John lowered his foot, leaned elbows on knees, and put his fingertips together in a teepee shape.

"Let's not kid ourselves. We both know why she's making such a fuss over me." Patrick sipped his drink and with a chunky finger wiped away a trickle of sweat along his temple. "It's my inheritance."

"Surely, you can be wrong about that. Why...I'm sure she finds you very...um... interesting. After all, you helped start this amazing industry. That's got to mean something. Shelley, I mean, Miss Auburn, may be overbearing but she isn't..."

"She isn't what?"

"A fortune hunter." His voice squeaked as he forced out the words he knew to be a lie. Seemed Shelley would hunt down anything she wanted if she thought it was in her best interest.

Patrick shook his head and laughed with sarcasm. "Nice try, padre. Look at me. I'm short and chubby. Even my mother finds me repulsive. We both know the truth about Shelley. The question I have is, what do I do? Should I go along with the façade? After all, she's a beautiful woman. That's something you don't have to lie about, right?" He winked.

John's face burned.

"Never mind. You don't need to say anything."

"What do *you* think you should do?" In seminary, he learned that a rhetorical question was always the best way to weasel out of a situation where one didn't have an honest answer.

"I've no idea. That's why I came to see you. I could pretend she cares for me and marry her, knowing full well she doesn't. Or I could call her bluff."

"Do you love her?"

Patrick lowered his feet from the table. "Can't say that I do. She's beautiful, of course, but if she's shallow enough to want me for my money, she'd be shallow enough to take every penny once we've said, 'I do.'"

"You've got a good point."

"That's it then." Patrick plunked the glass on the table and stood.

"What?"

"I'm telling her to get lost." He waddled to the door. "Thanks, padre."

"Wait a minute..."

The door opened and closed and Patrick Malloy was gone.

Chapter Three

SHELLEY GLANCED AROUND the lobby to be sure no one was watching. She held up her Blackberry, *click,* and took a selfie with the large Universal Station logo in the background of the shoot.

She wanted to capture the moment. *All of this is going to be mine soon.* Patrick was hours away from proposing. By tomorrow, she'd post this picture on every site known to mankind.

"An evening at the Ritz tonight." Shelley spoke to the phone and smiled at her image. "Getting everything you've ever wanted, girl. Mom and Dad would be so proud." She tapped the phone to silent and slid it into her Gucci Soho shoulder bag —a recent gift from Patrick.

"Shelley?"

"Um. Hello, Missus Malloy."

The petite, five-foot framed woman dressed in a black suit approached Shelley with powerful assurance. The wrinkled skin above her brow creased with a question. "What were you doing?"

"Just admiring the new logo."

The towering shield had four separate quadrants. Top right

were two M's intertwined for the Malloy name, top left were four stars to demonstrate the small beginnings of the idea, bottom right a picture of the globe, bottom left the company's emblem.

"It's quite impressive if I say so myself." Marjorie Malloy smiled.

Shelley turned toward her. "Was there something you needed from me?"

"Actually, yes." She placed her hands on Shelley's arms. "I have a huge favor and I know I can rely on you." Marjorie squeezed.

"Anything." Shelley's chest puffed. This woman would soon be her new mother-in-law, and one day she'd be the one asking Marjorie to do *her* favors.

"There's an urgent request from our headquarters in London. They need to have someone with total access to the database get there straight away. I told them I had the perfect woman for the job." Marjorie released Shelley's arms.

"Certainly, Missus Malloy. I can be ready by Friday."

"Actually, you'll be leaving in two hours." She clicked her heels like a general demanding attention.

"What?" The harshness in Shelley's voice was stronger than she intended. She rubbed her cheek with the back of her hand to remind herself to calm her tone. She'd learned that trick from her mother. "I couldn't possibly be ready in such short notice. Besides—"

"It's already a done deal. Yours and John's tickets are waiting for you at reception. Go home, pack a bag and get back here in one hour."

"John?"

"Yes. John Cox. I hope you don't have any concerns with him traveling with you? I never send any employee alone on a trip. You know that. There's too much at stake."

Shelley tried the sugary approach. "What about Patrick? He could go with me."

"I need him here." Marjorie Malloy's tone flattened. "Please don't question my decisions. I could've sent any number of people, so be flattered I chose you." She did an about face and headed to her office around the corner. The waft of strong perfume lingered, faded and followed her retreating back.

"You sound relieved." Shelley brushed her hair at the same time she informed Patrick on the phone about their change of plans. She had rushed home, threw a bag together, made arrangements for the neighbor to keep an eye on her house and finally contacted him to cancel their evening date.

"Uh. Not really. When mother wants something done though, she gets her way."

"You're right about that." Shelley pressed her lips.

"Enjoy yourself."

"Goodbye, Patrick. I'll miss you."

"Sure." He hung up.

She shrugged at his flippancy and flicked off the bedroom light.

Shelley picked up the plane tickets and headed to John's office. "Guess you have to put up with me for a few days, huh?" she crooned, as John opened the door.

"How in the world did I get chosen for this privilege?" He gathered a few things from his desk and snapped a briefcase closed.

"I don't know. But it sure messed up my plans. Big time."

She strode to the window and glanced at the view. The rain had stopped. Any remnant of snow had melted into oblivion as masses of people trudged to work along the Mall, umbrellas held over their heads offering little protection against Mother Nature's buffeting wind. "Wow. Someone's taken good care of you. You've got the best view in the building. Even Marjorie doesn't have a panorama of the Lincoln Memorial like this."

Shelley returned to John who stood by the door, his hand on the knob. "Are you ready to go?"

She pecked his cheek as she walked past emphasizing the swing in her hips. "This should be fun."

"Fun isn't quite the word that came to my mind."

Shelley swung back, her satiny, red skirt swishing with the movement. "Did you have something else in mind?" She tapped his cheek with a polished nail and dragged it gently and slowly along his dimple.

"Words like...boring, tedious. Those were the ones that came to mind."

"What?" She pulled away. "What's that's suppose to mean?"

"I hate flying, you and I have nothing in common, and I won't have anything to do except follow you around like a pup while you take care of business with whomever at some office. That's what it means."

The elevator opened and they entered silently.

At the ground floor, a taxi waited and they quickly settled inside.

John looked out the cab's window as the driver pulled into a gap in the traffic and headed toward the airport. Fortunately, the rain had eased. "It's going to be a very long trip if we choose not to speak to each other the entire time."

"I would *hate* to disappoint you and your expectations. I'll make this as boring as you can possibly imagine." Shelley hissed.

"I—"

"Look, John." She turned to him. "I don't like this any better than you do. I had grand plans for tonight. Patrick was going to ask me to marry him. I'm sure of it." She faced front, and pouted with crossed arms. "Everything I've been waiting for...put on hold for a lousy trip to London. With *you*."

"Hey, I'm sorry. Okay?" John touched her knee, then jerked back as if he had touched fire. "I'm sorry about your evening. And I'm sorry it's me going and not Patrick." He lowered his voice. "I'm sorry about what I said earlier, too. About this being tedious."

Shelley looked at him. Her brimming eyes dried quickly. "It's okay. We'll still have fun, won't we?"

"Yeah, sure. Fun." He looked out the window and frowned at his reflection.

Chapter Four

"WHY ARE YOU so upset?" John pulled his carry-on luggage into the wide-aisled first-class section as Shelley trailed close behind.

"These long delays seem to happen more in D.C. than any other airport. Makes everyone grumpy," she growled.

"To include you?" He lifted the bag to the overhead compartment then proceeded to place hers next to his.

"I'm not grumpy. I'm focused."

"Oh, that's original." He chuckled under his breath.

"You take the window seat."

"Yes, ma'am." He caressed the fabric on the seat with the gentle stroke of a pet owner with a new kitten. Thanks to Shelley and the elite status with the airline carrier, they were the first in line to board the plane. Seconds after they were seated, the stewardess handed them a crystal flute of sparkling champagne.

"Wow. I've never flown like this before." The effervescence tickled his nose.

"Welcome to my world, John." Shelley clicked the glass with his. "Haven't you ever traveled for U.S.?" She slipped off crimson high heels, leaned back and stretched out her long legs.

"Only short jaunts between D.C. and New York on those tiny commuter jets that even sardines avoid."

"Believe me, there's no other way to fly than this." Shelley curled her toes and released them. "We'll wake up in London as if we've been at home in our own beds, asleep. Only tonight, we're sleeping together." She gave him a gentle nudge in the ribs and pursed as if to kiss him.

John was sure someone held a torch to his feet. Heat seared up his legs and out his arms. "Shelley," he croaked.

"Yes?" She leaned in and fluttered a sensual bat of her eyelashes.

"Stop. Please. Don't tease like that. I'm not a prude. And I've told you before, I do find you very attractive."

"So what's the problem?" She moved in, closing the gap between them. Her scent permeated his body like a dry sponge dunked into a bucket of warm water.

He backed away and cleared his throat, his shoulders pressing the cool, oval window. "The problem is, I also respect you as a woman. Don't change my opinion of you by acting like this."

Her face crunched into a childlike grimace. "Oh, I forgot, you don't tease Mister Padre. You're too holy."

"I'm not holy. I have feelings like every other man. I'm just asking you not to behave like you're a spoiled teen, and we'll get along great."

"Fine." She leaned back, the leather embracing her like an oversized coat.

The plane's engines revved and with a slight jerk the large jet moved in reverse from its parking slot and headed toward the runway. An announcement filtered through the speaker system: "Ladies and gentlemen, welcome to flight 1909 to

London, Heathrow. For your safety, please give the attendants your undivided attention." The stewardess went through the emergency drills. When finished, the attendants found their seats for takeoff and within minutes the plane had reached altitude.

John eyed Shelley. She clutched the chair arms with white knuckles and her eyes scrunched closed. "You okay?"

"I'm fine." She grimaced. "Takeoffs are the worst."

"Ah. So you don't like flying either?"

She cracked one eye open and peeked at him. "Not really."

Lights for seatbelts turned off and lavatory signs lit up. She sat straighter, released the seatbelt and smoothed her skirt.

He smiled. "Let's start over, shall we?"

"Start over with what?"

"Getting to know each other. Without the flirting or that girly stuff you keep trying on me. I don't really know that much about you, other than the short times we've chatted at the office. Tell me about yourself."

"There's not much to tell." She fingered the chair. "Grew up in New York. My parents were lawyers. I'm an only child. End of story."

"Are your parents still in New York? Do you see them often?"

The stewardess interrupted their conversation. She now wore a white apron attached to the front of a starched, pale blue uniform. "May I get you a snack? We have a fruit and cheese platter or salmon slices and cream cheese on melba toast."

"Nothing for me, thank you," John said.

"I'll take both," Shelley smiled at the stewardess, "and I'll take his, too, I'm famished."

John leaned in and whispered, "That'll cost a fortune."

"It's free, silly." She giggled.

When she laughed, Shelley's eyes sparkled like the champagne in his hand. He shook his head to rid the thought. "Then I'll take mine. I'm hungry, too."

"It's beautiful." John gazed out the window as the stewardess picked up the last of the dishes and glasses off their trays.

"What?" Shelley leaned across him and peered out. "Oh, it's only the sun setting." She settled back and flicked open the airline magazine.

"It's *only* the sun setting? Really? That's all you see?"

"Sure." She shrugged and flipped to another page. "I don't know what you think you see."

"I see hot lava pouring from the volcano of heaven."

Shelley lowered the magazine. "Wow. You are a romantic if I've ever heard one. Lava? Really? Corny, if you ask me." She picked up the magazine again.

John's faced burned like the reflections on the clouds. "I happen to think it's better to see the world through rose colored glasses and marvel at the Creator than to think this is all purely accidental and not worthy of amazement. Look." He turned to the window. "It's magnificent."

She gazed out again briefly. "Sure. It's nice. But give me Universal Station and the possibilities of its expansion and I'll show you creativity and beauty."

John slid the window shade down and took a deep breath, stemming his frustration. "So you didn't finish telling me about your family in New York. What's it like growing up in the Big Apple?"

"No big deal. Like growing up anywhere else. Where did you grow up?"

"Small town in South Carolina. Summerville, to be exact."

"Never heard of it." She tucked the magazine into the slot

alongside the chair and grabbed a blanket and pillow. "Now we'd better get some sleep. Tomorrow's going to be a busy day."

"It seems to me you don't really want to talk. You're willing to tease and joke about sleeping together, but when it comes to sharing anything about your life you shut down."

"What do you want to know? I told you there isn't much to tell."

"You said you don't have any siblings. How about pets? Did you have any pets growing up?"

Shelley focused on a place just past John's shoulder as if remembering a better time. The slight smile made her appear ten years old.

"What is it? What kind of pet did you have?" He prodded.

She returned to the present. "Well, I wanted a Great Dane. But in an apartment in New York, that wasn't about to happen. So I had a hamster instead."

He chuckled. "That's not a pet. That's a snack for a quick cat."

Shelley slapped his arm. "That's not funny."

"You're right." John ran his hand down his face, wiped the wide smile off and managed straight lips and a solemn gaze. "In fact, my best friend growing up had a hamster. Everyone on the block played with the thing. Then tragedy struck."

"What happened?" She leaned forward with intense interest.

"Brownie—that was the hamster's name—was flattened when my friend's little brother sat on it by mistake. We were all there when it happened. The kid insisted, with heartbreaking sobs, that his mother try to 'bring it back to life.' Their mom was a bit weird, but she loved her kids and would do anything for them. So, she gave the hamster mouth to mouth resuscitation."

Shelley's eyebrows rose, and skepticism reached from her chin to forehead as she sat back. "You're making this up."

"No. Really." He crossed his chest with his finger. "Cross my heart. I'm not making it up."

"What happened?"

"The hamster was *too dead* to revive. When she blew into the hamster's snout, something inside kind of made a popping noise."

"Ugh. That's gross." Pursed lips told him she was fighting not to laugh.

"Actually we thought it was kind of cool—at the time. Boys have a strange way of looking at the world."

"That's for sure."

"Somehow, though, boys manage to grow up and become adults who contribute to society."

"Hmm. Most of the time."

John crossed his arms to stop the sensation of chills running up and down his spine from her engaging smile. "So what was your hamster's name?"

"Henry. Henry the Eighth." She giggled.

"Okay. I give. Why Henry the Eighth?"

"We kept bringing in females to breed and they either died or he attacked them. We gave up after eight of them. And we never managed to get any babies from Henry. But he was mine and I loved him." Shelley sighed and pulled the blanket closer. "Are you satisfied?"

"About what?"

"You now know something not even Patrick knows about me. Not that he'd be interested in my childhood anyway."

"I'm sure he'd be fascinated. Just give him a chance."

"Sure. The heir of U.S. fortune interested in my hamster named Henry. Now that's something to laugh about." She hit the switch and turned off the overhead light. "Now if you'll excuse me, I've got a busy day tomorrow after I wake up from sleeping with you all night." She smiled, rolled to her right side and covered her arm with the rest of the blanket. "Good night, John."

"Good night, Shelley."

Chapter Five

SHELLEY EXITED THE first-class lavatory and returned to seat 3C. "Drats." She bent, retrieved a rolling lipstick tube that had dropped to the floor, and stood on tiptoe to return her cosmetic bag to its proper place within the large carry-on.

"What's the matter?" John rubbed his eyes. He touched the light button on his watch. "Why are you up? It's the middle of the night."

"It's not the middle of the night in London, silly. It's morning and we'll be landing soon."

He lurched upright and ratcheted the window shade up. "How can that be?"

Bright light burst into his face. "Ouch." John tucked his face into the crook of his arm. "Think I had too much champagne or something."

"It's called jet lag."

He looked up. "Wow."

"What?"

"How can you look that amazing so early?"

"It's a gift." She fluffed her hair with her fingertips.

He smacked his lips and mouth as if to rid a nasty glue taste.

"Some of us aren't so gifted. It takes a pot of coffee and a long hot shower for me to even begin to feel human, never mind be—"

"Be what?"

"Never mind."

"Why, John, I do believe you were going to say I'm beautiful. Or was it gorgeous? Doesn't matter. We both know it's the truth, but it's still nice to hear."

He cocked his head. "You're sincere, aren't you?"

"Of course I am." She sat next to him and buckled in. "Thought a *man of the cloth* would respect honesty."

"Wow. You're too much. I've never met anyone quite like you. Vanity is not necessarily an appealing quality you know."

"I'm not vain, just aware of my assets. Besides, who cares if it's appealing or not? I *am* attractive and I use it to my advantage, that's all."

"I'm beginning to wonder if I had you all wrong." He brushed his fingers through his hair and a few strands stayed upright.

Shelley forced herself not to pat the hairs back in place. "In what way?"

"I thought underneath that façade of superiority and over-ambition existed a woman of depth and character. Think I was way off base."

"Think what you like. I know what I want from life and I have no problems getting it with the gifts I've been given."

"You mean like snagging an innocent bystander like Patrick and drawing him into your web of deception. You've no more romantic interest in that man than you do to a tick on a dog, do you?"

Shelley clicked her tongue. "Honestly, you are the most naïve man I've ever met. Every person is out for themselves, to get what they want, however they can. Even you. How are we really any different from each other? You use God to get ahead in the world. Look at that office you have. You can't say it isn't something to brag about."

"I feel so sorry for you, Shelley. You have such a strange outlook on life and distorted view of other people. The only question I have is, 'why?'" He turned toward the window and touched the glass. "Maybe we should keep our conversations to strictly work-related topics."

She choked back a response and forced tears to retreat, the hidden hurt squeezing her insides with the tenacious hold of a shark. She straightened the chair to its upright position and clenched her jaw shut.

"The Hyde Park Hyatt, please." Shelley and John crawled into the back seat of one of London's vintage black cabs.

Better be nice to John. I might need him someday to help with Missus Malloy. She's a hard nut to crack. Yet she seems to like him.

She cleared her throat and placed a hand on his. "You've been awfully quiet."

He slid his hand away. "I've nothing to say."

She shrugged, leaned forward and spoke to the cabbie. "I've never quite figured out what the fuss is all about. With the weather here, I mean. Every time I've come it's been pleasant. Even this time of the year."

"Give it ten minutes." The driver snickered as he pulled out. "Clouds are already moving in." His Cockney accent was a male version of *My Fair Lady's* Eliza Doolittle.

Shelley tilted sideways to view the airport. "Heathrow's enormous. Terminal Five has to be the largest in the world."

"They're planning on expanding, too. Load of rubbish, if

you ask me." The cabbie slammed on his brakes, avoiding a lorry blocking traffic.

Shelley jerked back. The velocity of the cab forced her nearer John. She touched his knee and smiled.

"Let's keep to our own space, shall we?" he snarled.

"Sure." She moved away.

"First time in London?" The cabbie looked at John in the rearview.

"It is for me."

"Shall we take him past Big Ben and the Parliament building?" Shelley asked.

"No problem." The driver put on his blinker and moved over a lane.

"See on the right, across the street, that's Saint Paul's Cathedral." She leaned across John and pointed out the window.

John shuffled closer to the door. His negative body language of crossed arms and legs expressed a thousand words. "Looks like something from a postcard."

"Come on, John. Let's dispense with our differences and enjoy the scenery. If it's your first time here, you'll want to experience it. It's a beguiling city."

"What's the plan for the day?" he muttered.

Shelley moved back to the other side of the cab. "We'll go to the hotel, get settled and then I'll head to our headquarters near Piccadilly Circus."

"What time will we leave?"

"You don't have to come with me. I'm perfectly capable of getting there on my own. You rest and then go and take the red double-decker tour bus around London. Enjoy yourself."

"No way. I've strict orders to be with you wherever you go."

"Look. I'd prefer you not come with me. It'll be our little secret. Besides, you'd be bored stiff."

"Doesn't matter. I'm coming with you. That's why

Marjorie Malloy paid big bucks for my ticket to come here. Not so I could sightsee."

"Fine. Be ready by eleven."

He looked at his watch. "Great. That gives me a few hours. I might even get in a run beforehand."

"Hyde Park is just across the street from the hotel," the cabbie interjected. "There're plenty of people who run or cycle there, but don't carry any valuables. Gypsies'll nick anything they can get their hands on."

"Thanks for the advice."

The cab came to a halt in front of a white Victorian building, complete with colonnades.

John stepped out from the taxi, Shelley following. "Thank you."

The cabbie tapped his forehead with a salute as she handed him a large tip. "Cheers."

A doorman, dressed in black top hat and long tails, directed the porter to their bags and they proceeded to the open-planned lobby.

"I need to travel internationally for U.S. more often." John gazed at the foyer, where paintings of red-coated, foxhunting horsemen hung on the walls. Behind the reception area, a picture of Queen Elizabeth in full regalia graced the room. Recently crowned, King Charles' portrait hung beside his mother's.

Shelley slipped her hand into the crook of his arm. "Stay with me kid, you ain't seen nothing yet." She winked and snapped at a porter who guided them to a private elevator that took them to the fourth-floor suites.

"See you at eleven." John swiped the electronic key and opened his door.

"See you then." She disappeared into the hotel room across the hall that would be home for the next several days.

Chapter Six

JOHN BRACED HIMSELF for the frigid outside air. "Shelley thinks it's nice. I say it's freezing." The hotel porter gave a quizzical look at him and his verbal ramblings.

Dressed in well-worn jogging gear, he smiled at the top-hatted porter, stepped out of the lobby and onto the street.

Crossing the road where yellow flashing lights stopped traffic for pedestrians, he took a quick jog through a turnstile and entered Hyde Park.

Stopping momentarily, he blew into cupped hands and read a large billboard sign with a detailed map of the park. A winding trail traveled next to a water park and alongside the Princess Diana Memorial Fountain. Miniature Christmas lights draped from tree limbs and lamp posts. "Whoa. This place is massive."

The quiet rhythm of his paced footsteps was soothing as John's muscles relaxed with the tempo of his run. Pebbles crunched underfoot and he moved onto the paved, designed trail. *The brochure in the hotel room said the Greater London area has nearly four hundred parks. Can't imagine they're all this beautiful.*

He picked up speed, circled a large portion of the park for forty-five minutes, and headed back to the hotel. Retrieving his key, he caught the elevator and opened the door to his room.

After a long hot shower he just might be able to deal with Shelley's shenanigans.

Rap. Rap. Rap. "Shelley, it's John. I'm ready whenever you are." He glanced at his watch. 10:50. "I know I'm early." John pressed his ear against the door. "Shelley?"

He returned to his room and called the operator. "Can you please ring Shelley Auburn's room?"

"I'm sorry, sir, there's no answer."

"Can you tell me if she's left the hotel?"

"I'm sorry but I'm not able to say."

"Why not? I'm her traveling companion and I need to know if she's gone. I may have misunderstood when and where we were supposed to meet." *Does a small white lie count in these circumstances?*

"I'm sorry but it's against hotel policy to release any information about our guests. It's strictly for security reasons."

He slammed the phone down. "Security. I'm going to *secure* Shelley to a phone booth and lock her in there."

John flicked on the television and BBC News ticker-taped the headlines as a Scottish woman with Middle Eastern features reported the weather. "Today it's mostly cloudy, with some periods of sunshine. Temperatures are around five Celsius—that's forty-one Fahrenheit."

He paced the large room until he was dizzy, stopped at the window and looked down. A bright red phone booth, an iconic United Kingdom trademark, appeared pencil-sized on the sidewalk below. Umbrellas popped open and traffic moved at a steady rate. "Guess the cabbie was right when he said the clouds would roll in."

He slapped the windowsill with a hard crack. "I *cannot* believe she left without me. I've no idea how to find her. Wait until I get my hands on that pretty throat of hers."

John's reflection revealed deep lines of anger. "Lord, please help me restrain both my frustration and desire for Shelley." He let out a long breath, inhaled then exhaled as if to clear his lungs of filthy air and his mind of conflicting thoughts.

"Guess there's nothing I can do right now but wait." He sat on the edge of the bed and flipped through the Sky Channels.

Ring. Ring.

He leapt to grab the phone. "Hello?"

"Hello, John."

"Shelley?"

"Miss me?" She giggled.

"*No.*" He slammed down the phone. "Now why'd I do that?"

Ring. Ring.

"Don't hang up on me." Shelley firmly ordered.

"Why shouldn't I?"

"Because you wouldn't know how to get a hold of me, where I am, or how to tell Marjorie you lost me in this grand city."

"Why'd you leave? You tricked me so you could get out of the hotel while I went for a run." If he were a Rottweiler, he'd be growling with the best of them.

"I didn't trick you. You just wouldn't listen. There was no point in you joining me this morning, but I couldn't talk you out of it. And I knew this would happen."

"What happened?"

"The idiot I was supposed to meet is out today. Called in sick. The reason we have so many problems with our company here is that the CEO doesn't have a clue he needs to be in the office for the thing to run. This has happened more than once when I've visited. The Malloy's are going to hear about this as soon as I get back to the hotel."

"When will that be?"

"Well, there's no point in me coming back right now. It's only five thirty in the morning in the states, so I couldn't reach her anyway."

John gritted his teeth. "So what are you going to do?"

"It's what *we're* going to do."

"What would that be?"

"I want you to catch a taxi and meet me at the Tower of London. We're going to play tourist for a few hours. Then we'll go back to the hotel and I'll call Marjorie. What do you say?"

"*Sayonara*. That's what I'd like to say."

"I didn't know you could speak multiple languages." Shelley giggled again. "Come on. Let's have some fun. There's nothing else we can do about this right now. Besides, you should thank me."

He grunted. "Why would I do that?"

"I saved you from a boring morning, you had a great run, and you didn't have to follow me around like a pup. Remember you said you thought this was going to be a tedious trip? I wouldn't dream of letting that happen."

"Where do you want to rendezvous?"

"That's more like it. You'll find me at the little outdoor café right across the street from the entrance to the Tower. Meet me there."

"Fine."

"And John?"

"Yes?"

"Try to enjoy yourself, will you? I don't want to hang around a spoiled sport when I could be having fun with friends at a pub."

"Is there anything else?" He growled deeper.

"See you in twenty minutes. Don't be late." She hung up.

Chapter Seven

"THERE YOU ARE." Shelley waited at the entrance to a retro café. She brushed a kiss across John's cheek, motioned him to join her at a table she'd procured inside by the front window and sat. Pictures of the Beatles, 60's paraphernalia, and a red Mustang's bumper served as a backdrop. A plastic red rose was propped in a clear vase. "What would you like to drink? Latte? Do you want something to eat? They serve breakfast all day here if you're interested."

She offered him a menu. "You must be hungry after your run."

"You're insufferable." He slumped into the chair across from her.

"Why? What have I done? I just offered to buy you a coffee and a meal. That should count for something." She smiled her best Angelina expression, hoping to diffuse his anger. Generally, it was very effective.

"Don't give me that look of innocence." John slapped the table. "You know precisely what you've done."

People at nearby tables stopped talking and looked their way.

"Please lower your voice, darling." Shelley waved slightly and beamed at those who glared at them. "This is England. Not Macaroni Grill. Folks expect quieter conversations here."

John gritted and whispered harshly, "I am *not* your darling."

She leaned in and whispered back, "Fine."

"Why did you leave without me this morning?"

Shelley sat back and clicked a full water glass with her nails. "I've already explained why. Besides, it's over and done with. Nothing was accomplished and I promise you can come with me tomorrow and help strangle that CEO."

"Did it ever occur to you that maybe he didn't want to see you?" John poured himself some water from a ceramic carafe covered in musical notes.

"No. That's silly."

"You said this happened before. That he's not been around when you've arrived."

"Yes. But that doesn't mean it's because of me." She swirled the ice cubes then sipped the water. Truth be told, she'd wondered if the imbecile at the office was afraid of her. "Anyway, let's just enjoy ourselves. You've never been here before, and it's a rare occasion for me to get a chance to be a tour guide. Normally, I come, I conquer, I leave."

"What makes you think I want a tour?"

"Give it up, will you? Being angry is not a very God-like way to behave. Besides, you're too sweet to stay angry for long."

"Can I ask you a question?" John leaned back in the chair.

"Shoot." She winked.

"Why do you insist on being so difficult? As if no one or nothing matters? I can't believe you're really that hard or self-centered."

"Believe what you want. They don't call me Hard as Shell for nothing."

"Is it me, or are you this way with everyone who tries to get close? Including Patrick? If so, your marriage will be as shallow as that glass of water."

"What business is it of yours?"

"Because I happen to think underneath that bravado of yours lives a woman who just might be hurting."

Arms tightly crossed, she tightened her lips. "I've worked long and hard to get where I am. I'll ask you not to try and analyze my motives."

A waiter, dressed in an open-collared shirt and black trousers, came to their table. "Are you ready to order?" He opened a small pad, pencil poised.

"Full English breakfast for me and an Americano," she replied. "What will you have, John?"

"I haven't even looked at the menu. What's a full English breakfast?"

"It's eggs, toast, hash browns, sausage, bacon—otherwise known as rashers, tomatoes and baked beans."

"Baked beans for breakfast?"

The waiter laughed at John's puzzled look. "Sorry, mate, our tastes are a bit different, but as they say, 'It's tradition.'"

"Go on, give it a try." Shelley touched John's wrist and he jerked away.

"Make it two full English." She handed the menus to the waiter. "Plus two Americanos."

"Thank you. I'll put this order in straight away."

"I can order for myself." John glowered as the waiter retreated.

"I'm sure you can. But the meal is my treat, so relax and enjoy the view of the castle."

John's eyes flickered interest at the Tower of London's reflection in the dark River Thames. "I've heard so many stories about that place." He spoke toward the castle rather than her. "Always imagined it'd be like this. Never thought I'd actually be sitting here and see the real deal, though. It's amazing." He looked back and spoke with tenderness. "Look. I'm sorry. Okay?"

"You're forgiven."

"Don't you think *you* owe *me* an apology?" John's tone escalated.

Shelley lowered her eyes. "It's very rare, but you're right. I was wrong to fool you and leave the hotel." She looked up at him. "Do you forgive me?"

"Are you sincere or is this another act?"

"I am *very* sincere. Now don't push it or you'll never hear me say those words again."

"Fair enough."

The waiter brought two steaming platters nestled in the crook of his arm, placed one in front of John and the other in front of Shelley. He returned with two mugs of hot coffee.

Shelley lifted the cup in a toast. "Here's to a new beginning for us. What do you say?"

John clinked his coffee mug with hers and spilled a few drops. "New beginnings."

"That's the best breakfast I've ever eaten. Even the baked beans taste different here than at home." John sipped the last of his drink, wiped his mouth with a napkin and placed it on top of the now yoked plate. "The eggs were fantastic."

"Told you you'd like it. When are you going to learn to trust me?"

"When you start acting trustworthy."

"Touché." Shelley placed the fork down.

"Sorry, that was uncalled for."

"No. You're right. I haven't been very nice, and I want to

change that. Let me pay the bill and we'll head across the river. You'll love the Beefeaters."

"Another restaurant?"

"No silly. That's the name of the guards that watch over the Tower."

"I've got a lot to learn."

"And I'm just the girl who can teach you." Shelley paid the bill and took John's arm as they headed across the river to England's notorious fortress.

Chapter Eight

JOHN AND SHELLEY peered through the glass, following behind a long queue of tourists, and viewed the secured relics dating from the fourteenth century.

"No jokes." He laughed, as they were pressed tighter together by the increasing crowds.

"Now what makes you think I'd say anything?" Shelley giggled as they continued to move slowly along the display of the finest regalia in the world. "...about the family jewels, that is?"

"They're the *Crown* jewels."

"You know I couldn't resist." Her smile was natural, not the fake smear of a grin she often wore.

He ribbed her with an elbow. "Can you imagine wearing that thing on your head?"

"I'd like to be the Queen and give it a try." She winked.

The twinkling in her eyes caught him off guard, and the scent of lavender, roses or some other flowery aroma surrounded her with a sensual cloud.

"You okay?" Concern swept across her face.

He swallowed hard. "I'm fine. Why do you ask?"

"You just got a funny look on your face, that's all."

Gulp. "It's nothing." He whispered. *Nothing that is, except the desire to press my nose into your hair cascading along your neck and shoulders.*

The noise around them seemed to fade, and they were caught in a capsule of connectivity. They drew closer, their faces nearly touching, their breath intermingling.

"Patrick." He choked.

"What?"

"I'm thinking about Patrick right this minute."

"I'm not."

He stepped back as much as the crowd allowed, and the noise level increased. "I know. Me neither. Not really. But I need to remember you were expecting the man to ask you to marry him only yesterday. I need to honor that. And you."

"Thank you for being such a gentleman. I think."

They shuffled along the museum's aisle as the crowd began to disperse into the next room. A group of international visitors hovered in a nearby corner with a private tour guide. John and Shelley maneuvered around the masses.

"Can I ask you something?" John guided, his warm hand on her back, toward another exit.

"Again? Every time we're together you want to ask me something."

"You are the most complex woman I've ever met. Questions are the only way I can find out if the person you are pretending to be is the real you."

Shelley rolled her eyes. "Go ahead. Eventually you'll get tired of this game and realize I'm nothing more than what I appear to be. Then you can move on to the next person you think needs spiritual intervention."

"Do you actually think that's why I'm interested in you?"

"What else could it be? You've already told me we have

nothing in common. I want to take over U.S. and be the next CEO. You want to save those who are lost." Shelley's face remained passive.

"I've upset you."

"Not really. Let's go find a place to get a cup of coffee. The crowd is starting to make me feel claustrophobic."

They wove through several rooms, found an elevator, pushed the button, and arrived on level three. John pointed. "There's a table over there. You grab two seats and I'll get the coffee. Latte okay?"

"Perfect."

Shelley gave John a brief wave as she sat. He returned the gesture and jumped in line behind a host of others vying for food and drinks. John was by far the most attractive man to honor the room with his presence. Her back still tingled from his touch.

"Cut it out, Shelley. Cut. It. Out," she murmured. "Do not complicate your life with him. All the pieces are falling into place with the Malloys."

"Did you say something?" John set the tray on the table.

"Um, no."

John shrugged with nonchalance. "I bought a couple of star-shaped shortbread cookies to go with our drinks. What with Christmas right around the corner."

"Cookies are called biscuits here. I'm not usually into sentimentality or holidays." She pulled a cookie toward her. "But I'll take it."

"This is amazing."

"Are you talking about me again?" Shelley giggled, bit into

the pastry and it crumbled onto the tabletop. She brushed them into a pile.

"No, not this time."

"What then?"

"I'm talking about the people. They're from all over. I've seen Asians, Middle Easterners, overheard Americans speaking, and I think someone said they were from Nairobi. I love it."

"What's the big deal? Universal Station has employees from everywhere, too. We have to hire them in order to have our global influence."

He waved a large arc. "Everyone's in the same room and no one cares where others are from. They're just enjoying the experience of the Tower and respecting each other. No one's pushing or getting angry. It's a little bit of—"

"*Mommy!*" A wail resounded around the large opened dining area and pinged over the heads of customers. Murmured voices, clatter of utensils, and sounds of the diners came to an abrupt halt.

"What's going on?" Shelley stood. "Sounds like a child's separated from her parents. Somebody has to do something."

"*Mommy.*"

"Please, someone help her." Her eyes filled and she fidgeted with a napkin, twisting and turning the paper until it tore.

"It's okay." John touched Shelley's wrist. "Look, her mother's found her already." A woman dressed in tight jeans and denim jacket had scooped the child into her arms and cuddled her. "See. Everything's okay."

The hair on the back of her neck settled. "Good. I'm glad." She sat and dabbled the corner of her eye with the napkin.

"What was that all about?" John cocked his head.

"What?"

"Seems to me you overreacted a bit when that lost child screamed."

"It's nothing." She pulled away.

"I think it was. Want to talk about it?"

"No. Thanks. Let's just eat our cookies and finish the coffee." Shelley pushed the plate away. "On second thought I think I'm finished. We should probably head back to the hotel." She stood and walked away.

Chapter Nine

ICY PELLETS PATTERED THE roof of the black taxi with the beat of a timpani stick on a kettledrum. Storefronts and neon pub signs blurred as traffic crawled along Constitution Hill.

Honk. The driver slammed on his brakes to avoid a moped that slipped between the taxi and another vehicle, nearly hitting the bumper of the small cycle. "Sorry." He looked in his review mirror at Shelley and John, who'd been jolted. "Lousy weather makes for lousy traffic."

"It's okay." Shelley shrugged. Raindrops dribbled down the taxi's window and flicked to the curbside joining ever-growing puddles.

John cleared his throat. "Do you—"

"No. I don't want to talk about it." She hardened her tone. Her set jaw restored self-control. "Ever. Understand?"

"If you say so. But—"

"There are no buts." With crossed arms, she peered out the cab window. John couldn't possibly understand how deeply the lost child's scream had affected her. He probably had never felt abandoned in his whole life.

John waited for Shelley and leaned on a counter near the concierge area. The lobby swarmed with business people carrying black briefcases and wearing dark suits.

Ding. A family of tourists, obvious by camera bags the size of small suitcases, trailed out of the elevator. Each wore heavy overcoats. The parents and five trailing children gathered by the door. Coats and maps were passed around before they launched outside.

Ding. John glanced back at the elevator and assessed Shelley as she approached. Dressed in a chocolate tailored suit, she was the epitome of a corporate executive. The beautiful hair he'd admired earlier was now pulled in a tight bun, and brown-framed eyeglasses gave the effect of intellectual astuteness.

He smiled. "You ready?"

"Let's go," she ordered. The tough exterior was firmly in place.

"Yes, ma'am." He stood upright and his smile faded.

Shelley held an iPad in one hand and an iPhone in the other. "I'll ring Missus Malloy on the way to our office on Piccadilly."

"Fine." He followed her along the foyer.

"Once we get there, you can wait for me in the executive suite. There will be refreshments and books if you need something to do. This shouldn't take too long."

"Okay."

Shelley stopped mid-step and turned. John almost rammed into her. Her cheeks were puffed with angry air. "You sound like a robot with your answers."

"And you're acting like one." John cupped his mouth. "Sorry. That slipped out."

"Earlier you said you wondered who I really am." The

crystal eyes hardened to diamond rough. "What you see is what you get."

"Are you sure?" He stepped closer. "Because the woman I was standing next to at the Tower was a softer, gentler one than..." He scanned her up and down. "Than the dressed-up robot who's pretending to be so tough."

With gritted teeth, Shelley poked his chest. "Don't ever try to figure me out, or feel sorry, or try that God thing on me. I've done perfectly fine on my own for the past ten years and I'll continue taking care of myself, thank you very much."

His hand twitched and he clutched his fingers into a fist. *Then why do I want to grab you and hold you?* "I'm sorry you feel that way." He stepped back. "So Miss Auburn, tell me what you need me to do and I'll be glad to assist however you wish."

"That's better." She exhaled. "Please get us a taxi and give the driver the address. I'll finish with my call and we'll be on our way."

"That was quick." John rose as Shelley entered the executive suite of the London U.S. office building.

"The idiot still isn't here. Wait until I call Missus Malloy again. She's going to go ballistic." The fire in Shelley's eyes could light wet wood.

"Calm down. I'm sure there's a logical explanation."

"I think you were right." Shelley threw a briefcase on a table and slumped in an overstuffed chair.

"Me? About what?"

"The guy *is* afraid of me."

John sat and tried keeping his tone even. Maybe if Shelley stopped responding like a John Deere bulldozer with men she wouldn't have an issue with the guy. "Is there something you can do to rectify that, do you think?"

"Yes." She sat upright.

"Good. What is it?"

"Fire him!" She jumped up, determination on her face like a soldier facing the enemy.

"Shelley, that's not what I had in mind."

"You asked if there was something I could do. I can do this."

He stood and held her arms. "I meant was there something *you* can do to make the poor man stop hiding like a frightened Chihuahua."

"*How rude.*"

"You're right." He backed away, hands up in surrender. "Keep acting the way you are and you'll have everyone thinking you're scarier than their worst nightmare. That'll get them to do their jobs better."

"I'm not going to tell you again, John. Stay out of my business. Now if you'll excuse me, I've got work to do. Take a taxi back to the hotel. I'll meet you there later. We will head home tomorrow—a day early."

"Oh, yeah, that's right. We need to get back to Universal Station. You've got to get your claws into Patrick. Heaven forbid he'd discover you're just using him to get what you want. Maybe I'll give him a call and warn him of the impending danger."

He left Shelley with a gaping mouth and a look of horror.

Chapter Ten

"I'M AFRAID FLIGHTS aren't departing or arriving into Heathrow for the next twenty-four hours," the young, red-faced male clerk behind the desk informed Shelley and John the next morning. "I'm very sorry, madam."

"What do you mean, they're not leaving?" Shelley spewed the words like projectile vomit. "They've got to be. There must be some kind of mistake. I need to get back to the states."

"Calm down, Shelley. It's not his fault." John put his briefcase on the counter. "Can you please explain what's going on? No one mentioned anything yesterday afternoon when we said we were checking out today."

The morning lobby was filled with suitcases and groups of hotel guests murmuring discontent. Intermittent breezes relieved the stuffy air when the glassed front doors automatically opened for foot traffic.

"There's been a disruption in transatlantic travel, and it's keeping flights from taking off and landing."

"I've heard of these kinds of things happening," John sympathized. "It occurred in 2020."

"But it's not supposed to erupt when *I'm* flying." Shelley

leaned on the counter and put her face closer to the clerk, teeth grinding. "Do you understand?"

The desk clerk tucked his chin in like a plebe at a military academy. "Umm. Yes, madam. However, I'm not the one making the decision."

She stepped back and waved like a madman. "The sun is shining. Have you not looked outside?"

"The disruption isn't necessarily because of the weather. We've no idea why it's happened."

"Ugh. Very well, have the porter take our bags back up to our rooms then."

"I'm...I'm sorry, madam."

"What about now?" She gurgled.

"Your room has already been booked by another guest. When you called last night and cancelled your stay for this evening, we reassigned them to someone else."

Shelley slapped the desktop. "You fool."

"I'm sure we can work something out, right?" John's tone was like cocoa butter on a hot burn for Shelley and the young man as the clerk turned his attention to the iMac on his desk.

"Let me see what I can do." He clacked the computer keys and glanced at Shelley every so often as if to be sure she didn't have something to throw at him. "I do have two rooms."

"We'll take them." Shelley slammed a credit card on the counter.

"But—"

"There are no buts. I said, *we'll take them.*"

"Shelley, will you let the poor guy finish what he's trying to say?"

"Spit it out, then." She huffed.

"The rooms are not the suites you are accustomed to, that's all."

She flicked fingers in the air. "Doesn't matter."

"Let...him...finish..." John's firmness startled her.

"Fine. Hurry up. I need to call back to the states and let our company know we won't be there until tomorrow."

The clerk cleared his throat. "What I was going to say was, the rooms are single beds, and have been smoking rooms previously."

"Ugh. I hate smoking rooms. No matter how hard you try to rid the odor, it's still there."

"I'm sorry, madam."

"Will you *stop* saying that?"

"Yes, madam."

"So?" John urged with a humorous tone.

"What?" She faced him. Her nose nearly touched his chin.

"Are we taking the rooms or not? If we don't, I'm sure others in this crowd will jump at the chance. We can just sleep in the lobby."

"Of course we're taking them." She slid the credit card across the counter into the clerk's hand. "You're lucky I don't get you fired."

John chuckled. "That's two men you've wanted to fire in the last twenty-four hours. Is that a record?"

"Why do you think this is so funny?" Shelley drew closer to him and snarled.

"Because for once, Shelley Auburn is not in control of something."

"*How dare you.*" Her tone deepened and she lifted herself on tiptoe, bringing their faces within centimeters of each other.

John leaned in, his lips nearly touching hers, and whispered, "How dare I what?"

Shelley dropped down from her toes and sputtered. "Nothing. Never mind." She spoke to the clerk, "Have the porter take the bags to our rooms."

The clerk's mouth lifted slightly, and she noted a slight twinkle flashed in his eyes. "Yes, madam."

"Now what are we going to do?" John lifted his briefcase and followed the porter and Shelley down the hall.

"I don't care what *you* do. I have to contact the Malloys, then the airlines to rebook our flight for the earliest one in the morning. We can meet up for dinner and discuss our travel plans for tomorrow." The tempo of her words matched the march in her step.

He smiled and faked a salute behind her.

Shelley spun around. "Aren't you going to say anything?"

He slipped his lips to a frown and lowered his arm. "No need to. You've got it all covered."

The porter stopped at a small door on the right at the end of the first-floor hallway. "What are we doing here?" Shelley shouted.

"This is your room, madam." He unlocked the door with a swipe of a key.

"There has *got* to be some mistake. I know that it's a single, smoke filled hole, but this is right next to the kitchen for the restaurant. Where is *his* room?" Shelley pointed to John.

"Don't worry about me, Shelley." He dangled a credit-card sized room key between two fingers. "I'm right next door if you need anything. Just tap lightly on the wall. Oh, and have a good day. I, for one, am going out to enjoy a beautiful day in the sunshine."

Chapter Eleven

JOHN SWIPED HIS brow with the towel draped across his shoulder. December seemed unpredictable. Yesterday it'd been damp and freezing. Today it was mild, and he had quickly broken a sweat after the first mile. Another four miles meant he was keeping up with the routine he usually maintained at home. Dodging dogs in Hyde Park, traffic along the road in front of the hotel, and hordes of people walking to and fro was a feat comparable to playing the Rally X arcade maze game with his dad when he was a kid.

He slid his hotel key into the lock and released it. Yesterday's rain showers had dissipated and bright sunshine spilled on the bed and dresser with a checkerboard effect. The odor of smoke lingered but was tolerable. This basic room of pine furniture and compact space was more of what he was used to when he traveled. Not the posh suites Shelley expected.

John muttered all the way, from the dresser where he'd slung the towel, to the closet where he pulled out clean clothes, and headed to the bathroom shower. "Shelley's so spoiled. I'd like to turn her over my knees and give her a good spanking. Her parents should have done that a long time ago. She's such a prima-donna."

He stopped mid-step, moved to the wall and pressed his ear against it. *Sobbing? Is that Shelley sobbing?* He pulled away. "So what. Serves her right."

John went into the bathroom, flopped his clothes over the towel rack, and turned on the shower. A quick look in the mirror and he stopped in his tracks. His face sported the usual five o'clock shadow even though it was only midday. *Who are you, John Cox, that you would be glad to hear a woman cry?* The words seemed to come from within, his conscience slapping him with a proverbial bowl of ice water.

"She deserves whatever she gets," he replied to his reflection.

You don't really believe that.

His shoulders slumped as he leaned on the sink. "No. I don't." He straightened his back and leaned in towards the mirror, growling at himself. "But, I'm having a really hard time being very sympathetic right now. She plows through life like everyone should kowtow to her. Telling that poor guy at the front desk that he was somehow to blame for the planes being delayed. How ridiculous was that?"

Go over and find out what's wrong. His conscience prodded.

"No!"

Now.

"Later."

Now.

"Ugh. There really are times I wish I'd never heard about God, or went to seminary and become a spiritual counselor." He made a face at himself.

You don't mean that.

"Okay, okay. I don't mean that." He turned off the shower and went back into the room.

John threw his sweat clothes on and grabbed the room key. "I only hope I don't regret this."

Doesn't matter what she says. You need to do the right thing.

"Okay. Stop bugging me now, will ya?" John spoke to the thin air as he closed his door.

He rapped on Shelley's bedroom door.

"Who is it?" she muffled from within.

"Me."

"What do you want?"

"I want to...want to find out if you're okay."

The door flung open. Shelley's eyes were red, face blotched, and clenched fists sat on her hips. She'd changed from her business suit to a furry pink sweater and brown yoga pants. Her hair tumbled around her neck and clung to her temples.

Even in distress she's beautiful.

"And why wouldn't I be?" Her jaw was set.

"I thought I heard—"

"What? Are you listening through the wall with a glass or something? You're worse than a girl. Mind your own business." She slammed the door.

He stomped back to his room, took off his sweats, grumbled on the way to the bathroom, turned on the shower, and avoided his reflection.

John scrubbed his hair with intense digs to keep his conscience at bay. "She is so darn frustrating." He washed his body and let hot water rinse the soapsuds off into the drain. "I want to strangle her."

You can avoid her all you want. But, you can't avoid Me.

He dried himself rapidly and put on black slacks and Beatles T-shirt—a gift he'd gotten himself when he and Shelley had gone to the café by the Tower. Then pulled a sweater over his head and yanked it at the waist.

"*Ugh.* She doesn't want to talk to me anyway. Besides, I

already tried asking what was wrong." He stood at the mirror over the dresser and continued his dialogue. "I can't do any more than that."

John clicked the remote in hopes BBC would drown out his thoughts.

Nothing but a talk show, just like in America. And Jerry Springer. The host interviewing a guest asked, "So tell us what happened?"

An attractive girl choked on heaving sobs as she dabbed her eyes. "I was so alone in a hotel room. All I needed was someone to listen to me."

He clicked off the remote. "Can't even escape with the TV."

John paced the faded carpet then stopped by the window. This room gave a closer view of people rushing around the building than the fourth-floor suite they'd had the day before. London was indeed a beautiful place. History spewed forth from every brick in the ancient buildings. A man and woman passed by with a baby in a stroller. Another young man and girl stopped, embraced and kissed. *Fairy tales. All of them.*

He yanked the curtains shut.

You can't block out the truth.

John pulled the curtains open. The young man and girl were gone, the stroller and parents no longer in view. *Sigh.* "Okay. I'll try again, Lord. This time help me, will ya?"

He found the room key buried under his dirty clothes and towel, took a deep breath, stepped into the hallway and rapped gently on her door.

SHELLEY HELD HER breath. *Go away.*

She tiptoed to the door and listened. John had obviously left.

It was quiet except for the noise of traffic outside the window. A car alarm blared. Shelley clapped her hands over her ears and lay facedown on the bed. "*Stop.*" The sound ceased and she released her hands. *I can't believe I'm stuck here.*

She rolled over, got up and paced the room several short laps. "I'm going to go crazy if I don't do something."

A wet face cloth, a little blush, and brushing her hair restored some control and settled her nerves.

Rap. Rap.

"I know you're in there," John said.

He is so stubborn.

"Can we talk?"

"Leave me alone." She stood her ground, waiting to hear his retreating footsteps. After a few more minutes, she carefully opened the door a crack.

John popped around the doorframe. "Just checking in on you."

"You're acting like a stalker. Go away." She moved to shut the door.

John stuck his foot in the doorframe and prevented it from closing. "Ouch. That hurt." He hopped on one foot, a crooked grin held at bay.

"What did you do that for? I told you to go away."

"I want to talk to you." John rubbed his shin. "Besides, you owe me a cup of coffee or something for almost breaking my leg."

"How do I owe you for something you did to yourself?"

"Are you really that heartless you won't offer a wounded man a warm drink?" He gave a hurting dog look, lips downturned and head tilted, hoping on one foot.

She flung the door open. "You're so troublesome. Come in."

"Thank you."

"Don't thank me. You forced your way in here."

John ignored the comment. "It's awesome how hotel rooms in England come complete with kettles, teabags, and snacks. Wish they did that in the States." He snatched a wrapped chocolate-chip cookie, plopped onto the only seat in the room, a rather worn green plaid armchair. "Smells like pasta or something in here. Been cooking?"

"It's the staff fixing lunch meals in the kitchen." She bloated her mouth and cheeks as if to throw up. "Smells like cabbage."

"Bummer."

"Do you want tea or instant coffee?" She topped the kettle with water from the bathroom sink and clicked the *on* button.

"Coffee's great."

"Did you go for a run?" Shelley opened two packets of instant coffee and shook each in a cup.

"Yes, but, I won't be able to run now for a month." He rubbed his ankle and moaned.

"Such a wimp." She added hot water to the cups, handed him a mug and sat on the corner of the bed cross-legged.

"More like a wounded bird. But I forgive you." He winked and sipped.

"You're insufferable."

He set down the drink and curled the right corner of his mouth. The lock of hair she always wanted to fix flopped over his right eye.

"Let's see. So far you've called me a stalker, a wimp, troublesome and insufferable. Did I miss anything?"

"Overly dramatic and slightly annoying. It doesn't appear that you really hurt yourself. You were just using it as an excuse to get in here." She watched him over her coffee cup trying not to succumb to his charm and 007 Daniel Craig manliness. "What *do* you want, John?"

"A truce."

"Fine. Now finish your coffee and go back to your room."

"What kind of truce is that?"

"What do you want me to do, draw blood?" She grimaced.

"Sure. I'll prick my fingertip—"

"I was only kidding."

John drew his brows together and tapped his fingertips. "Let's get serious for a minute, can we?"

"I'm generally nothing but serious."

He sat back. "Hmm. Now that's true. Okay, how about I get serious then and tell you what's on my mind once and for all?"

"Is that how it's supposed to work with a spiritual advisor? I thought you were supposed to listen, not talk."

"Well said. But in this case, I can't seem to get you to share what's really going on. So, can I be honest?"

"I would expect nothing less." Shelley took her cup to the

tea tray and sat back down. "Do you want any more coffee before we start our counseling session?"

"This is not a counseling session. Let's just talk as friends, can we?"

"Friends?" She forced herself to swallow and push back tears that begged to climb and spill. "Not too many people refer to me as...as a friend. I can think of only one person, really."

"I'm sorry to hear that. But, I'm sure you consider your parents friends, don't you?"

Shelley lowered her eyelashes. "My parents are no longer living. They died in a house fire years ago."

John's face whitened. He brushed the hair out of his eye and lowered his pseudo-wounded ankle. His tone was tender and soft, "I'm so sorry."

She shook her head and clutched the bedcovers under her knees so as to not reveal the building tension. "Thank you. But, it was a long time ago."

"Doesn't mean it doesn't still hurt. I can't imagine not having my parents around."

"Yeah. It was tough at first. But, I'm made of thick hide."

"If that's so...why were you crying earlier?"

She stiffened. "I don't believe that's any of your business."

"If we're friends, we have to be honest with each other. Something's going on that's making you so difficult—putting up this shield of having it all together. Then crying behind closed doors."

Shelley jumped from the bed. "If it's all the same to you, I'm perfectly happy the way that I am. And if you are a *friend,* you'll accept me for who I am."

John stood, ran his palms along her arms and took hold of her hands. "I *am* your friend. As such, I want to help. You were upset earlier. What happened?"

The tears escaped like a burst pipe. "If you must know, I

spoke to Patrick earlier. He's broken our engagement even before he conjured up the courage to propose."

John pulled her closer and let her cry on his chest. "I'm so sorry."

The fresh smell of soap and cologne seeped into her nostrils like hugging a clean sheet that had just come off the clothesline. Shelley stepped away and wiped away the tears. "It's all right. Really. I don't know what came over me."

"It's called pain. Embrace it." He handed her a tissue from a soft travel packet on the dresser.

"No. Pain hurts. Strength endures." She grabbed the tissue. "If Patrick doesn't want to marry me, I'll survive."

"Surviving is not living. It's keeping your head above water so you don't drown. Let your heart plunge to the depth of sorrow and you come up stronger than you ever imagined."

"Easy for you to say."

"Not really." John sat down. "There's a lot you don't know about me. Obviously, there's a lot I don't know about you. Why not put the kettle back on and let's have another cup of coffee. Who knows how long we're gonna to be stranded here. We might as well make the most of it and get to know one another better."

Shelley clicked the *on* button, settled back on the edge of the bed and crossed her legs.

Chapter Thirteen

THE MORGUE-TYPE silence in the room made Shelley squirm. John's laser stare forced her to lower her eyelids.

"Ahem."

"What?" She picked at bits of fabric off her yoga pants.

"Are you going to stare at your clothes all day, or are we going to get to know one another and start talking?"

"You start." She avoided eye contact and watched the digital numbers on the side table clock.

"Okay." John rose and went to the window, his back to her. "I'm a dreadful spiritual advisor." Daylight encircled his frame and glowed like a full body halo.

"Wait a minute. This is not going to be a bash-myself-up session, is it? If so, I'm not very good at that game."

He turned and leaned on the windowsill. "Of course not. Just trying to be honest, that's all."

"So, why did you say you aren't a good spiritual advisor? With what I've seen, I'd beg to differ."

"I'm saying that because I've had my own experience with pain when it could have been avoided."

Shelley uncrossed her legs, set her feet on the carpet and leaned toward him. "Are you saying you can avoid pain? That's hard to believe. There are things beyond your control that you can't change." She sat back and closed her eyes trying to block out the memories of her parent's death that had paraded across the news for days after it happened all those years ago. She'd only been a child.

"You're right. There are things we can't control. But, there are many things we can."

She opened her eyes and returned to the present. "For example?"

Rap. Rap. "Hotel service."

Shelley jumped from the bed and opened the door. A petite woman with tired eyes stood outside. Her broken English defied understanding. Only the motion of her hands gave her intentions that she wanted to clean the room.

"Do you want to go out for a walk and continue our talk while the room is being straightened?" Shelley asked John.

"Sure. I'll go and grab my coat."

"Let's go see St. Paul's Cathedral and then the decorations along Brompton Road in front of Harrods. They're usually spectacular."

"Not much into holidays, huh?" John cooed.

She ignored his ribbing. "When we get back, I'll have to call Missus Malloy and then the CEO at Piccadilly. I need to see if I can finally make contact with *that man*. He's probably cowering under a desk somewhere waiting for me to show up, fire him and shove him out the door." Shelley yanked a black overcoat out of the closet and barked, "Stupid guy makes my blood boil."

"A walk will do you some good then." John touched her shoulder, looked at her for a few lingering moments and smiled with chocolate mousse sweetness. "Let's get out and enjoy the day and continue our conversation, shall we?" He headed toward his room.

Too bad you weren't on the Titanic, John. Your charm could've melted the iceberg.

"It's magnificent." John stopped on the steps of St. Paul's Cathedral. The domed structure held a commanding view of the azure skyline. Wisps of feathery clouds pointed like arrows to the spire jutting out of the dome.

"I don't think there's a place in the world quite like London." Shelley stood close enough that their arms touched. He might as well have stuck his finger in a 220-electric socket. The sensation would probably feel the same.

She turned to him. "This sits on the highest point in the city and is the seat of the Bishop of London. The Bishop performed Kate and William's wedding in Westminster."

Shockwaves of connection drew them closer. John swallowed slow and hard. "I didn't know you were a royalist?"

She smiled, shrugged and moved away, breaking their contact.

"Guess there's some girly girl underneath that tough skin after all?" He winked and gently took her elbow and guided her up the steps.

"I've only been in here one other time and it took my breath away."

The massive dome and arched columns inside rose ahead. Large, ornate candelabrum lined the aisle and illuminated golden statues and paintings. "It was dedicated to St. Paul the Apostle in AD 604," Shelley whispered.

"You're remarkable," John said.

"Now why's that?"

Her electric smile hit him again. He spoke softly as they continued walking the long aisle. "One minute, you come across meaner than a rattlesnake. The next, you talk about Kate and William like every girl who wants a fairy tale ending."

She shrugged. "Got to keep men on their toes, don't I?"

"No wonder the CEO is hiding under the desk." He laughed softly, and they continued toward the ornate altar. "It's breathtaking. Thanks for bringing me here."

"You're very welcome. It's a place every spiritual advisor needs to visit to rejuvenate their call in helping others."

"You're right. This has been good for my soul. Now what's good for yours?" They stopped beneath a marble statue of Mary holding the crucified Jesus across her lap.

"I'm not sure." Shelley walked away.

John caught up with her. "Let's finish looking around here, grab a sandwich and have a picnic in the park. What do you think?"

"It's pretty cold for a picnic. But, let's do it. We can find a sheltered bench. There's a *Pret A Manger* takeaway just around the corner. I can order a pickle and goat cheese on a baguette. It's one of my favorites."

"Ugh. That sounds awful."

Shelley's tinkled laugh rippled along the archway. A tall man, hat dangling in his hands turned toward them and put a finger to his lips. "Shush."

"It's time to go, we've upset the natives." She giggled again.

"You're going to fall running down the steps like that," Shelley yelled after John as they exited the front of the cathedral.

"I'm in a hurry. Can't wait to try the goat and pickle." He waited at the bottom of the stairs, hands on knees, panting.

"I might be unpredictable, but you're crazy."

"Hm. A *crazy* spiritual advisor. Now that's a title to be proud of."

Shelley slid her hand in the crook of his arm. "You're darn right it is."

Chapter Fourteen

"SO WHAT WERE we talking about?" John swallowed a large bite of sandwich. He shoved his hand into a salt and vinegar potato chip bag and retrieved a handful.

"When?" Shelley shooed away a football-sized pigeon eyeing her food.

"In the cathedral. Remember? I asked you what *you* did that was good for your soul? Since you took me to Saint Paul's for mine."

The pigeon brought two more fellow birds along to join the harassment party. "*Go away.*" She waved at them. The birds flapped their oversized wings and flew to a nearby fence.

"I work." Shelley pulled off the bread crusts and tossed them toward the fence. The three amigos dropped below, grabbed the crumbs and flew off with a sluggish takeoff. "It's good for me. Keeps me level-headed and focused."

She turned to him. "I know that doesn't sound very spiritual, but it's how I cope."

"With what?"

"With life."

He crumbled the chip bag and put it inside the empty takeaway paper sack. "Do you mind if I ask you another question?"

"Can I stop you?"

He chuckled. "Nope."

"Go ahead."

"Tell me what happened with your folks. How old were you when they died?"

She straightened and the back of the park bench shifted slightly. "The fire happened in a resort in the Catskills while they were on vacation. One day we were laughing together at home. The next day they drove off to celebrate their anniversary and never came back. I was young. Twelve to be exact. Old enough to know what it feels like to be abandoned."

"Ah. That explains it." A gentle breeze threatened to swoop up the bag of trash and John grabbed it before it hopscotched down the path.

"Explains what?"

"Why you reacted the way you did at the Tower. When the little girl lost her mother."

"The feelings flare when I least expect them. I'm an adult now, and I need to get over being left by my parents."

"I'm so sorry. So did you stay in New York?"

"Yes. My grandmother took care of me when they left. So her place became my permanent home. She was such a wonderful woman." She tilted back and inhaled. "But, no one can take the place of your mom."

"That's for sure. No one can. But, friends can help fill the void a little bit, can't they?" He touched her hand and she didn't pull away. He clasped it tighter.

"Thanks, John." Shelley lowered her head and gazed at him.

If possible, he would stare into those eyes for eternity and never tire of the depth within the soul of their owner. He shook his head to refocus and stop gawking. "For what?"

"For always seeing the best in people."

"You're welcome."

"We'd better get back. Afraid we'll have to forego Brompton Road this time. I need to call the office. And Patrick."

He released her hand and stood. "Oh. Still trying to see if you can work things out with him?"

"I deserve an explanation at the least. He called, told me our relationship was finished, and hung up."

"Maybe this is one of those times pain can be avoided?" *You don't really love him anyway.*

"You mean I should avoid him?"

"No. But, why push the issue. It might just make it worse."

Shelley hailed a taxi when they arrived at the street. "I don't think it can get any worse than it is. Besides, I need to at least have a working relationship with Patrick. I'm determined to move up the company ladder regardless of what happens between him and me."

John bit his lower lip.

"What?"

"For just a minute...a split second...I thought the real Shelley was beginning to reveal herself. Now you're back to taking over the company. Is that really what you want?"

A taxi pulled up to the curb. John opened the door for Shelley and they climbed in the back.

"It's who I am." Shelley moved to the far side of the cab.

"I don't believe it."

"Believe what you want. I promised myself when my parents died that I wouldn't rely on anyone ever again. That way you control your destiny, and as you say, avoid the pain. If you're in charge, you don't have to worry about being hurt."

"So you'd hurt Patrick in the process of getting what you want? There's some inconsistencies with your theory."

She shrugged. "I wouldn't hurt Patrick. I'd make him into someone he wouldn't be without me."

John rubbed the top of his head and drew his hand down along the back of his neck. "I've never met anyone quite like you."

"Why, thank you. I feel the same."

"Hello, Missus Malloy." Shelley held the phone in one hand and waved a room service menu card in front of her face with the other. It didn't seem possible it was winter in England. The temperature on the television boasted twelve degree Celsius. This wasn't December weather. More like spring. She'd changed from the pink sweater to a short-sleeved khaki T-shirt.

"Yes, ma'am, I did speak to Patrick. I was going to call him next and see if he and I could talk again. He didn't sound like himself."

Missus Malloy babbled on as Shelley continued cooling herself. She moved to the window and half-heard the voice on the other end of the line. Information about the British CEO, what was going on in the Washington office and plans to open a new facility in Asia. Blah. Blah. Blah.

"Wait a minute. What did you just say?" Shelley reentered the conversation. Missus Malloy's tone had shifted gears.

"I said, Patrick's conversation with John Cox was insightful, I guess. Something John said to Patrick convinced him to postpone any serious relationship for the time being. I tend to agree with him. Patrick has some maturing to do. I know you understand these things."

Shelley visualized a slight sneer on the woman's face, the wrinkled brow raised in happy relief.

"I'm sure Patrick told you about his chat with John."

"Of course he did." She clamped on the bile growing at the base of her throat and offered her best light-hearted response. "But, I assumed it was with other girlfriends Patrick had. Not between him and me. We certainly need to clear this up."

"I'd leave well enough alone for now. In the meantime, get a hold of the CEO and persuade him to reengage the financial backers. We need to keep their bucks in our banks. If he's not up to the task, I may assign you there permanently."

"Thank you. But, I'm not sure I would want to live in England full-time."

"Let's discuss that only if the situation warrants."

"Yes, ma'am." She squeezed the phone. *Wait. Until. I see that John Cox. Think I'll pull that tempting little curl right out of his head.* She hung up and traipsed to the next-door neighbor's room. John wouldn't know what hit him.

Chapter Fifteen

RAP. RAP.

"Hey." John swung the door to his room wide enough to allow Shelley into his man cave. "What's...?"

She stepped inside and with a wide arced flat palm, slapped his face.

John cringed at its force and rubbed his cheek to soften the sting. "What was *that* for?"

"You talk about avoiding pain. Yet you inflict it without even thinking. You were right, though."

"About what?"

"You are a lousy spiritual advisor." Shelley spun, walked out of the room and slammed the door behind her.

The thin walls between the two rooms gave John ample opportunity for him to hear what Shelley really thought about him as she ranted from the other side.

"That woman is the most complicated creature known to man." He grabbed the edge of the dresser. "She's right up there with the platypus, a bunch of parts that don't match. I'm done trying to figure her out."

John dug a sweater out of his bag. "I need a long walk to

cool off. Otherwise I'm going to punch something." He slammed the door, stomped down the corridor and exited into fresh sunshine.

Shelley paced the room with the pent-up tension of a tiger trapped in a cage. She grabbed her coat. Outside the window, the sky was bright and inviting and she needed to cool off. Even though she and John had just returned from their trek to St. Paul's Cathedral, this time her jaunt wasn't for pleasure but sanity.

She slipped on the coat and fingered the pocket for the room key.

Ring.

The phone jingled. Patrick? No. The number was a U.S. extension but not one she recognized.

"Hello?"

"Miss Auburn?"

"Yes."

"This is Doctor Bosworth's office. Could you hold on the line, please?"

"This better be quick. This is an international call you're making."

"Miss Auburn? This is Doctor Bosworth."

"What's going on?" A lump of concern stuck in her windpipe and she gulped. "What can I do for you, doctor?"

"I wanted to let you know I've reviewed your recent blood work. Your platelet levels are quite low, and I'd like for you to come back for some further testing."

"I'm sorry. I'm currently out of the country and I'm not sure when I'll be able to return. Is this serious?"

"Please don't worry."

Doctors seemed to say those words with so little conviction.

"As soon as you're back home, call the office. We just need to retake the test and reassess your numbers."

"What are you worried about?"

"I'd rather not discuss this over the phone. But I'm sure we can come up with options as soon as we've narrowed down what's going on."

"Great."

"Miss Auburn. Please. Try not to let this bother you during your trip. We'll take care of things as soon as you return."

"Fine. Thanks."

Shelley hung up but instead of leaving she sat on the edge of the bed, held her stomach and tears flowed without prompting. First, Patrick broke off their engagement. John was the culprit who caused Patrick's decision. And now this. Where was her mother when she needed her? How many times had she cried out to the empty void her mom had left?

The silence confirmed her suspicions. Nobody heard her pleas. Nobody cared.

Shelley picked up the coat and held it close as if cradling a baby. She caught her reflection in the mirror and stiffened. "I've been on my own so long I should be used to it."

Her shoulders curved inward and she pressed her face into the coat. "But I don't want to be alone anymore." Why couldn't she find peace? Joy?

She straightened and spoke to her image. "Stop sniveling. You've overcome other things. This is just another bump in the road. It'll be fine."

She spun from the face she knew had lied. This was bigger than anything she'd ever faced. What was wrong that had the doctor so concerned? Who could she ask to help should she need it? *Talk to me like we're friends,* John had said. His words pierced. Could someone really care for her? Not John. He was a traitor and she couldn't count on his friendship.

The door popped as she exited the room and yanked it closed. Determination was her only friend and she was not about to let some clinical problem, nor John or Patrick for that matter, stand in her way.

Shelley stomped down the long hall to the front desk. "Is there any news on the flights resuming from Heathrow?"

"No, miss."

She slapped the desk, propelled around and ran smack into John.

He held her by the arms. "Whoa."

She shrugged his hands off and snarled, "Get away from me."

"You at least owe me an explanation for this bruise you've given me." John cupped his cheek.

"I don't owe you anything."

The rustle of paper from a hotel guest who sat in the corner on an overstuffed chair was an indicator that their conversation was traveling. John took her by the elbow and steered her toward the large Georgian window by the exit, away from the others and the staring eyes of the Royals in the pictures on the wall.

John released her elbow. "What happened when we separated earlier? We were having a nice time together. At least I was having a nice time. I thought you were too."

"That's before I found out you betrayed me." She formed fists and hit the side of her thighs to keep herself from slapping him in the face again. Anger was not helpful. Willpower and control. Those were her faithful companions. Always had been.

John stepped back as if she had hit him. "What are you talking about? I would never betray you." He reached out again and she pushed his hands away with her forearms.

"I spoke to Patrick. He's broken off our engagement. But that's not the kicker."

"It's not?"

"No. The real kicker is that Missus Malloy told me he was having a conversation with his spiritual advisor. You. And he was advised to break it off."

"You've got it all wrong." John's face shifted from consolatory to scarlet uncertainty. "Well. Mostly."

"What do you mean mostly?"

"He came to me for advice."

Shelley shifted onto the other leg, hands on hips. "Really? Now that's classic. Turn the tables. Patrick has no more interest in spiritual issues than I do. Why would *he* come to *you*?"

"Can we please go somewhere more private to talk about this?"

"Where do you suggest? There are hundreds of stranded travelers in here and there's no way we're going to find a quiet corner in this place. You're definitely not welcomed in my room for a cup of coffee so forget even asking."

"I wasn't going to ask. How about we go around the corner? I passed a Costa Coffee when I was out and it seemed pretty empty."

"You'd better have a conjured up good explanation why Patrick should come to you and why you would tell him to get rid of me by the time we get there."

"All I ask is ten minutes of your time without you hitting, shouting, or accusing me. Can I at least have that?"

"You don't deserve anything."

"You're right. I don't. But neither do any of us. We don't deserve anything that God has given us."

"I'll give you five minutes if you'll not use Him," she pointed upward, "as an excuse for your behavior."

"It's a deal." He held out his hand.
She shook it, squeezing as if to break each and every bone.

Chapter Sixteen

COSTA COFFEE HAD filled with patrons since John had passed by only an hour before. Customers were lined past the condiment stand and circular tables in the front section of the restaurant. Stuffy air combined with a smell of sour milk permeated the immediate area.

John pinched the bridge of his nose. What could possibly be worse than Shelley's aura of anger? Perhaps waiting for coffee with a bunch of uptight folks needing their legal drug of choice. "Why don't you go find a table and I'll get us something to drink? There's a seating section upstairs, maybe you can find two empty chairs."

"Fine." Shelley wove through the crowd and headed up the wooden stairs. The swing of her hips, swish of hair across her back, and step of determination flicked on a switch of desire in his soul's furnace. He waved his credit card in front of his face to diminish the flame. Shelley's persona had the seismic power of an earthquake, and he knew she was totally aware and proud of it. What a woman. What man could possibly tame her? Who would want to?

His coffee order placed and retrieved, sugar packets and stirrers in his pocket, John took his time heading up into the temptress's den.

John maneuvered around several small tables and caught sight of the back of Shelley sitting in the far corner. He approached carefully and placed a cup in front of her. "Great choice. We'll have some privacy over here."

He sat and sipped his drink and nearly burned his lip. John jumped up. "Shelley? Are you all right?"

Shelley's chin was lowered to her chest, eyes closed, and arms hung limply by her side.

A couple sitting across from them, who'd been staring into each other's eyes when he'd set down the drinks, must have noticed Shelley's lack of response. The young woman quickly came to his side. "I'm a part-time volunteer emergency technician with the British Red Cross. Is everything all right here?" She knelt next to Shelley's chair.

"She seems to have fainted or something. Will she be okay?" John moved back to allow the woman enough space to attend to Shelley. The noise in the restaurant halted.

"I have cold compresses in my bag for emergencies such as this." The young woman wiped a cool cloth across Shelley's forehead. "What a coincidence we happened to be in here during our break." The woman nodded toward her companion who'd joined them with a cup of water. "That's Nate. He's a Red Cross technician too."

"I don't believe in coincidences. I'm so grateful God brought you here when we needed you."

The two tilted their heads as if he'd spoken Greek. It seemed talking about faith in public was an anomaly.

Shelley released a low moan. She moved her head back and forth in slow motion as if to indicate 'no.' But she was in no state to realize what was going on.

"My name is Jean," the young woman spoke softly. "How're you feeling?"

"Light-headed. What happened?"

"We aren't sure. Have you had episodes like this before?"

"No." Shelley moaned quietly as if in pain.

"Are you hurting anywhere?" Jean went through the trained litany of questions and monitored Shelley's vitals with her fingers pressed on her wrist. "Your pulse seems a tad low but not dreadfully so. Would you like for us to call an ambulance?"

"That's not necessary." Shelley sat up slightly and pressed her palms against her eyes. "I'm sure I'll be fine."

Conversations around them picked up and normal chatter resumed.

Jean stood. "Nate and I will be here for a bit longer so let's see how you're doing in a few minutes. If you feel any different, please let us know."

"I'm so sorry to have bothered you."

"It's no trouble. I would suggest you see a doctor as soon as possible." She handed John a card. "There's a surgery around the corner."

"Surgery? She shouldn't need that, surely?"

Jean chuckled. Youthful lips, colored with dark red lipstick, were a stark contrast to the dyed pink stripes in blond hair. "What you would call a walk-in clinic, we refer to as surgery."

"Ah. Excuse my ignorance." John took the card.

"We are certainly two nations divided by a common language."

"What a clever thought."

"It's not original." Jean closed the small satchel. "It's attributed to Bernard Shaw or Winston Churchill, but no one knows for certain."

The young woman might have pink stripes in her tresses, but she had smarts in her head.

"Thank you again for your help. I'm not sure what I would've done if you hadn't been here."

John took Jean's place beside Shelley's chair and knelt to hold her hand. He caressed the top of it with slow tenderness. "Could it have been the heat? It feels like an oven in here after being out in the cooler air."

Jean said, "That's a possibility and could be from jet lag if you've recently traveled. Dehydration can cause lightheadedness. It's obvious you're not from around here."

"Obviously." John smoothed Shelley's wisp of hair away from her eyes. How he longed to kiss her pale forehead and hold her.

"If I may say so, it's obvious how much you love her." Jean nodded at John then toward Shelley.

John released Shelley's hand and stood.

Shelley bolted upright in the chair, straightened her hair and pulled at her skirt. "We're coworkers, not lovers," Shelley said sharply.

"My *coworker* is obviously feeling better," John's face burned and he resisted the urge to fan it again.

Jean and Nathan returned to their table, muttering something to each other about Americans and how odd they were.

John sat. "Are you sure you're okay?"

"I'm fine. Really. Don't make a fuss like a girl."

"You're insufferable."

"And you're a traitor."

"I guess you feel like yourself again? You don't miss a beat even when you get knocked down."

"Nobody knocks me down, John. Not you. Not the Malloys."

"Then why are you so upset with me for talking to Patrick? It's pretty clear to him that you want nothing more than his fortune."

Shelley took a sip of water. "If you must know, I thought we'd both gain something by our alliance. He'd have a wife. Someone who could help him become a better person. And I would have the company to take care of and grow to its full potential. So we both would come away winners."

"Funny."

"What's funny?" Shelley took another sip, her hand shaking as she placed the cup back on the table.

"Yesterday, I honestly believe you thought that. But something's different. There's not the same conviction in your argument."

"It could be because I just had a slight fainting spell." Shelley waved her hand as if to dismiss a servant.

"No. I think it's something more. What's happened today that has gotten you so worked up? It isn't just finding out about Patrick and me talking, is it?"

"Stop your spiritual digging, will you? You can't fix everyone's problems."

"So you have a problem." *Slow, John, slow.* Shelley was not one to rush into expressing deeper feelings. "Are you willing to tell me? I'm a friend. Remember? Not your enemy."

Shelley's eyes swam, the blue swirling colors matching the sea on a perfect summer's day. He clasped his hands to keep from grabbing hers, and lowered his head as he waited, giving her time. All the time in the world.

Chapter Seventeen

SHELLEY DABBED THE corner of her eyes with a tissue and took another sip of water. Coffee was normally her drink of choice, but with her head still throbbing and a nauseous stomach, water seemed to be the best option right now.

John's brown curl of hair spilled over his bowed forehead. Could he be trusted? After all, hadn't he told Patrick to break it off with her? Or had John just happened to be the listening ear to Patrick's usual flip-flop non-committal approach to life? Patrick found it difficult making a daily choice of what tie to wear, never mind who to marry. It was no wonder he was getting cold feet.

What was it about *this man*, one with the patience of a saint that was so different from the rest of his gender? She desperately wanted to believe in someone, something again. Could John really be the one she could open her heart to?

"John?"

He lifted his chin and the square jaw and fine lines around his mouth were Hollywood worthy. But it was the softness in his eyes, the thick brows furrowed as if he'd lost a puppy that drew her in. "Yes?" He reached across the table and covered her hand.

Ring.

Shelley's phone danced on the tabletop.

"Please don't answer it." John squeezed her fingers gently as he glanced at the phone. "Talk to me. Tell me what's going on."

"Just let me see who it is." She released his hand and checked the incoming call. "I'm sorry, John. I have to take this. It's Missus Malloy. She probably wants an update on the London office."

"Can't it wait? Just five more minutes." John sat back with crossed arms. The puppy look had now morphed into a forlorn child. The square jaw slackened with the pout.

"Hello?" Shelley turned slightly and lowered her voice. "Why, Patrick, how sweet of you to call." She winked at John and smiled coyly as she continued her conversation. "You didn't think I'd answer if I saw it was your number? Of course I would have. And I'm here now, aren't I?"

Shelley stood, held her hand over the receiver and said to John, "I'm going to take this outside so I can hear what he's saying. I'll be right back."

"Fine." John kicked the underside of the table, jiggling the coffee cups with its force.

John had been so close. He was sure of it. Shelley was about to divulge what was really going on. Patrick was just a diversion to cover the underlying pain she seemed to keep in check most of the time. For a brief second, he saw a crack in her protective armor.

Shelley returned with a cheeky smile and her controlled exterior back in place. "It was all a mistake." She sat, formed a pyramid with her fingers and tapped the tips together with delight.

"What was a mistake?"

"He didn't want to break off the relationship after all. I'm sure his mother is quite distraught over his change of mind, but she should be used to it by now. The man can't seem to decide what side his toast should be buttered on." Shelley picked up the coffee. Her previously shaking hands now clasped firmly onto the cup.

"It appears you're feeling better." Jean and Nathan stopped by their table. "Be sure to let your doctor know when you get back home that you've had a fainting spell."

"I will. I promise." Shelley nodded.

"Thank you again," John said.

"You're welcome. Enjoy the rest of your stay." The two of them left, Nathan guiding Jean away with his hand on the small of her back.

"I guess the fainting was just another attention-getter." John turned to Shelley. He kept his tone in check but could no longer control his words. He would do anything for this woman short of begging on hands and knees for her to be honest with herself and him. It seemed she was incapable of doing either.

"Why, John, how unlike you. To be so harsh, I mean. I'd have thought you'd be happy for me since I'm not angry with you anymore." She placed her hand over his.

He jerked away. "Stop. Just stop. I never know when you're putting on an act or being serious." His tone escalated in spite of every effort to keep his cool.

The coffee shop had slowly emptied, and the sun's fading light created prison-wall stripes along the far wall.

Shelley shrugged. "I've told you all along, anything I can do to get ahead and see my dreams fulfilled, I will."

"But why?" He leaned in.

"It's safe," she whispered and glanced over his shoulder out the window. "It's best when I'm in control." Shelley looked at him squarely. "Don't you see? As long as I can stay calm and focused then everything I've worked for will happen." She reached for his hand again. He put his hands on his knees to keep hers out of reach.

"What I witnessed a few minutes ago was a broken woman, unwell and frightened. Now I see one who'll stop at nothing to get her way. Even break a man's heart." John pushed the cooled coffee to one side.

"When my parents died, I decided then and there that the only way to live was to live for today. Who knows what tomorrow might bring? So why not get what you want from life however you can?"

"Did it ever occur to you that you aren't the only one who's had a rough time? Others get hurt, lose those they love and still move on without taking advantage of unsuspecting souls."

"What could you possibly know of what it's like to hurt so much you feel like your heart will never be the same? It seems to me you've been given everything on a silver platter. Mister Malloy spoiled you with that office of yours. I'm sure your family coddled you too." Shelley sat back with a smug look of conquest, a female warrior surveying her latest prize. All she lacked was a sword and sheath.

"You've no idea what I've gone through. You've never stopped long enough to ask. Ever since we left the states everything has been about you. How upset you were that Patrick didn't come on this trip instead of me. How the poor guy in the London office didn't jump when you walked into the building. You. You. You. You are the most self-centered, self-absorbed creature I've ever met. You're hopeless." John stood, the palm of his hands pressed into the table, leaning as far forward as he could.

Shelley stood and raised a hand. John grabbed her wrist and twisted it gently to one side. "That's your natural reaction. Strike out at whoever doesn't acquiesce to your needs." John released his grip. "Actually, I feel sorry for you."

He grabbed his drink and coat, left Costa Coffee and stepped into the cold air. The warm sunshine that had been shining when they'd entered was long gone. Outside wasn't the only thing that had turned bitter in a short amount of time. John bundled his coat under his arm and let the coldness penetrate his skin and inner being. Shelley was no longer going to determine his destiny.

John knew without a doubt what he was going to do once he returned to Universal Station. As far as he was concerned, they wouldn't get back to America soon enough to put his plan into place.

Chapter Eighteen

THE FRONT DESK was swarming with hotel guests when John entered the front lobby.

"Please. Everyone. Just leave your keys in the drop box. There's no need to formally check out if you've no outstanding bills from your stay with us." The concierge patted downward palms as if to calm the anxious throng.

"What's going on?" John stepped up to a short-stubby man with a pointed, bald scalp. With suitcase in tow, he was obviously another guest waiting for further instructions.

"Well, ole chap, it seems flights are beginning to take off from Gatwick and Heathrow and everyone's in a panic to get to their destinations," the man said with a thick accent.

"Thank goodness. I can't wait to get out of here."

The man's pencil thin eyebrows arched upward and formed a half circle on his forehead. "I do hope your time in England hasn't been so dreadful that you wish to leave in such a hurry."

"Oh, dear. No. I'm sorry. That sounded rude. It's just that I need to return to America to take care of business."

"What business would that be?" Shelley came up behind

him. "Getting back to Patrick and convincing him not to marry me?"

"I have no intention of doing any such thing."

John marched down the hall to his room and tossed trousers and shirts in the suitcase haphazardly. Unfortunately, he would have to spend time with Shelley going to the airport, aboard the plane for nearly nine hours, and on the ride back to the office. But that would be the end of it. No doubt, she would be as glad to see the last of him as he would her. She'd played him long enough.

Knock. Knock

Great. He was certain it was Miss know-it-all.

"What in the world's wrong with you?" Shelley, hands on hips, somehow managed to combine a sultry look with an innocent-teenaged-girl guise.

It was the same persona that had often troubled him and yet had drawn him in every time. "I'm getting ready to go. Haven't you heard? The flights are leaving."

"Yes. I know."

"Then why are you standing there so calmly? Aren't you in a hurry to get back and throw yourself at Patrick and fawn on Missus Malloy?" John went into the bathroom, packed his travel bag with shaving cream, razor and various toiletries.

"As much as I hate to say it and as much as I want to leave, I've some business I need to take care of before we go. I haven't spoken to the CEO in the London office."

He tossed the toiletry bag into the large case on the bed. "Fine. You take care of that and I'll see you on the other side of the pond."

Shelley stepped into the room. "You're supposed to stay with me, aren't you?" She moved closer to the bed. Instead of her normal directive tone, Shelley spoke with an even-tempered and kind voice he could hardly believe. "Besides, you're my travel companion, and you've been paid to be here. It's your responsibility to accompany me and leave this country when I do, isn't it?"

She was drawing him in again. The proverbial black widow to an unsuspecting grasshopper. What a fool he'd been. He slammed the top of the suitcase shut. "When do *you* propose we leave? Surely you can just call the CEO and sort this out over the phone."

"If I could've done that we would've never come here in the first place. This is a face-to-face meeting that needs to occur. I'll call him immediately and set up an appointment. In the meantime, please get our flight details sorted. We should be able to leave first thing tomorrow morning."

"Yes, ma'am."

Shelley placed a hand on his arm. "I never meant to hurt you. Truly."

"Don't give yourself so much credit."

She jerked away as if she'd touched a blowtorch. "Fine. Let's do what needs to be done and get back to Universal Station. I've a wedding to execute."

"Your future husband is the one who'll wish he'd been executed," he muttered as she closed the door behind her.

To Shelley, it was business as usual at the corporate office in London. The CEO had groveled toward her with the pathetic behavior of a schoolboy. The only thing missing were the short trousers British boys wore to primary school. Why Missus Malloy insisted this person should continue in this high paying position was beyond her. A robot could produce better results.

Shelley closed her leather briefcase and snapped the clasps in place. "I'm glad to see you have your inventory sorted and critical injunctions in place. I can return to Universal with full confidence in your handling of this important facility." It wasn't the whole truth, but she needed to wrap up their time in England and get back to work. Her real work. Taking over the company. Then she would replace this fool with a more qualified employee.

They shook hands, and Shelley exited the luxurious office with its view of the London Eye. The large, slow moving pods appeared to have stopped in space.

"Let's go, John." He'd been waiting in the lobby since their arrival an hour before. It was pure luck the CEO had still been in his office this late in the day, but it meant they could leave on the earliest flight in the morning.

"Yes, ma'am." John helped her on with her coat.

"Is that all you are going to say?" She looked into those sad eyes and wished she could somehow take away the pain she'd inflicted on this gentle man. Shelley was sure John was unaware of the influence he had on her.

From the first time she'd met him, she knew his integrity and Godly character could easily sway her from her ambitions. But she didn't want that. She needed to prove to herself she could fulfill her lifelong goals and not let some man thwart those plans. She needed to justify her existence, prove to her parents that she was worthy of the life they had given her. They'd lost theirs. Surely they would want her to make the most of hers.

"When we get back to the hotel I'll send our bags ahead to the airport so we won't have to wait as long to go through security."

"My you've become quite the travel agent in a short amount of time," she teased, hoping to ease the tension between them and somehow melt the ice statue's frozen heart.

"I'm here because I've been paid to accompany you. If I can

expedite our time here in any way, I will do my best to make that happen."

Shelley stepped nearer to John and could feel his warm breath caress her face. How had she managed to wound the one person who truly seemed to care? Could she really just move on with her life after the times they had shared; the picnic in the park, chatting over coffee, the tour of the Tower of London? She hadn't had that much fun since...since she couldn't remember. "John. I'm sorry. Really. Whatever has caused this rift between us, can we at least talk about it?"

"I'm afraid not. Shall I go and get us a cab?"

She stepped back. "If you wish."

John circled around her and went toward the office doors. The friendship that had begun to blossom between them had been crushed in the winds of her ambition.

Shelley buttoned her coat. Her future lay ahead, not with this man or the laughter and tears they'd shared. It was Universal and returning to Patrick Malloy. She stood straighter, threw back her shoulders and marched downstairs to the open door where a taxi waited for them to enter. Tomorrow was a new day of dreams realized.

She sat next to John in the back seat. He didn't say a word as the driver took them to the hotel and one step closer to returning home.

Chapter Nineteen

"THESE PEOPLE ARE crazy." John grumbled all the way through security. "Whatever happened to civility? Everyone's pushing and shoving as if it were the end times." He grabbed his computer bag and shoes from the screening treadmill and slid on his loafers as Shelley put on her wrist load of bangles and jewelry.

He couldn't wait to board, find their seats and get the show on the road. Chaos in the terminal had been mind-boggling with delayed flights and those needing to reschedule tickets.

John had had enough of England. He'd come with the hopes that this magical country of heroes, like King Arthur and the Prince of Wales would somehow forge a special relationship between him and Shelley. How idealistic could he have been? He was no prince and she was certainly no princess.

Boarded, seated and climbing through the clouds, turbulence on the flight was happening inside and out the metal machine. Currents of air slapped the aircraft back and forth until they reached a calmer altitude. The unsettled atmosphere inside the cabin was the one John couldn't comprehend.

Shelley couldn't have been nicer when leaving the hotel and

on their ride to the airport. Her courtesy toward him and others was so out of character he checked often to be sure she was the same woman. But he'd fallen for her trap too many times and would not be caught off guard again.

"Sir. Could you please bring us some champagne?" Shelley waved her fingers at the steward. The tall server, whose head nearly touched the plane's ceiling, brought two stemmed-glasses filled with sparkling drinks—a déjà vu of when they'd flown there.

"I'm not having any." John shifted. "There's nothing to celebrate."

"We're heading home, aren't we?"

"I suppose. But I'm still not having any."

"Fine. I'll drink it for the both of us." She smiled, the twinkling in her eyes like the reflection of a disco ball above a dance floor.

John stared out the window and shifted as close to the plane's wall as possible. He pulled a navy-blue blanket over his shoulder and closed his eyes. Sleeping would pass the time and keep Shelley from trying to converse.

Shelley was not about to let John spoil everything. He could sulk all he wanted. She was ready to get back, restart the clock in motion with the wedding, and take her rightful place at the organization's helm.

Her tablet opened, she began a to-do list: venue for reception, flowers, shop for bridal dress. Nothing but the best. Hopefully Patrick had already considered engagement and wedding bands. She typed it in as a reminder just to be sure. A wedding planner would probably be best so she could use her valuable time on more urgent matters—the office.

Was John really asleep or just pretending so he wouldn't have to talk to her? She closed the tablet and reached to shake his arm, but held back. What was the point? Maybe they could work it out when they got back to Universal.

Shelley flipped off the overhead light and curled into a fetal position. She might as well make the most of the time she had to rest. Every waking moment in the days ahead would be filled with preparations. Yet why did the knot in her stomach and uncertainty of this decision gnaw at her? She twisted and turned, trying to get comfortable.

The flight shuddered and bounced. Another air pocket created a jolt that startled her from near sleep.

John moaned and stirred. "What in the world's going on?"

She grabbed John's arm and clasped it with a vice grip. The overhead light dinged.

"Let go." John removed her fingers one by one. "I need to put my seatbelt on."

"What's going on?"

"I've no idea. I'm sure everything's fine. They just want to keep everyone in their seats. Now put on your belt and go back to sleep."

"Sleep? Who can sleep when the plane's going to fall out of the sky?" she spoke loudly and drew the attention of those on the other side.

A Scotsman, his brogue strong and deep, reached across the aisle and patted her arm. "Twill be fine, lassie. Just a wee bit of a bump in the clouds. All's well."

The steward came and knelt by her seat. "Are you all right, Missus Auburn? Can I get you anything?"

"My fingers and toes feel like ice." She shivered.

"I'm sorry you're frightened." John's tone was the soothing lilt of a parent to a child. "Everything will be okay. I'm sure of it."

The steward returned with two more blankets. Shelley draped them over her lap, patted her hair back in place and tried desperately to maintain some decorum. "Flying is the worst."

"So is taking advantage of others, and not being honest with ourselves," John whispered.

"I've tried to be as truthful with you as possible. For some reason you've had this idealized version of me in your head." She lowered her voice. "I'm sorry you're disappointed to find out it was a misconception on your part."

"You're right. I'd hoped the protective veil you've worn would be taken off, but you've become so accustomed to it there may be no hope of ever uncovering the true you." John turned again to the window and tightened his blanket.

To Shelley, they were two cocoons wrapped in their own little worlds.

The landing went without a hitch. John gathered their overhead bags and they moved with the herd down the ramp and spilled out into the terminal. A porter collected their bags and directed them to the waiting sedan.

"Please take us straight to Universal." Shelley dictated to the driver.

"Yes, miss."

He didn't want to talk, so they rode in silence until the vehicle pulled alongside the curb in front of the glass-domed building where Shelley wanted to reign as queen. She could have it all—the power, status, and money— and still be empty.

If only he'd been able to crack through her hardened shell he might have been able to make her understand. John shook his head and entered the building.

Without any goodbyes, they went their separate ways.

John took his bags to his office and closed the door. The view of the landscape was like being welcomed by the open arms of a lover. He stood by the large pane, placed his forehead and palms on the cool glass and closed his eyes.

"Thank you, Lord, that you have given me this place to work. Thank you that you've now released me from it."

As he walked around the desk, opened each drawer, and packed papers and office supplies into several small boxes he had in the closet. Unexpectedly, memories flooded in and his throat constricted. This had been his home for several years, but it was now time to say goodbye and move on.

John picked up the phone. The computer gave him twenty monotonic options before connecting him to Missus Malloy's office, and the answering machine clicked on. Perhaps it was better this way. He left a voice message stating his plans.

After hanging up, he placed the photograph of himself and Mister Malloy that sat proudly on his desk in his briefcase along with the first-print, leather-bound copy of *A Tale of Two Cities*. Mister Malloy was one person who had believed in him, and John would never forget his generous and gracious nature.

Once more, he picked up the phone and punched 0-1-0, this time for valet services. "Please ask a driver to come to the back of the building. I have several things I need to transport to my apartment."

This was the end of his shepherding, of carrying the title of spiritual advisor to a litany of computer geniuses who worked here. He'd indeed been blessed, but it was time to move on.

John picked up the box of personal belongings, exited and closed the door. This was a new chapter in Shelley's life. Time to put her behind him as well.

Chapter Twenty

SHELLEY LOCKED HER suitcases in the storage room and headed to the foyer. Her high heels clicked with energetic rhythm on the marble floor. Her spirit was buoyed by the dynamism of Universal Station's ambiance. There was no place like it. Life pulsed through its walls, and she was never more at home than here.

After her suitcases had been secured, she headed to the foyer. Once things were sorted with Patrick and Missus Malloy, she would go to John's office with a peace offering.

His friendship meant more than she was willing to admit. How could she repair the rift that had happened? Perhaps suggest enjoying a meal together before the wedding. She'd propose the wonderful Italian restaurant around the corner, and it would be her treat. Shelley picked up her pace.

Entering the cavernous entrance, where the ceiling skyrocketed upward of twenty-five stories, pervasive silence greeted her and the click of her heels echoed in the vast chamber.

Although most of the company's work was done behind insulated areas and enclosed data rooms, there was usually ample activity around the foyer and a constant buzz coming from various hallways leading to side offices. But the place was eerily quiet.

"Hello?" Shelley leaned over the front desk. Lights blinked on one computer and pictures floated on the screen saver of another. How odd.

"Hello, Miss Auburn." George, a security guard older than Methuselah and quieter than any man she'd ever met, touched her shoulder.

She jumped slightly. "You startled me."

"Sorry, miss."

"Where is everyone?"

"Not sure, miss."

"I'm looking for Patrick Malloy. Have you seen him?"

"No." He shrugged with abject ambivalence.

Shelley settled back on her heels, and placed her hands on her hips. "Is there anyone you know who's around?"

"Not seen anyone, miss."

"Never mind." She flipped a hand under her hair, clicked her way to the elevators, and pushed level ten.

Patrick could usually be found in one of the suites above the computer terminals eating his way through some god-awful pastry. That would most definitely have to stop in the near future. She'd help him see the error of his ways and get him on a treadmill as soon as she had a ring on her finger.

The elevator doors opened on the tenth floor. Utter silence permeated the landing and was indeed troublesome. Where in the world was everyone? A left turn down the corridor, another right turn and she'd arrived at the CEO's suite.

Shelley tapped lightly and turned the doorknob. Missus Malloy sat behind an oversized, lovely inlaid of pearl desk. Her head rested on crossed arms. Papers were strewn over the floor and the file cabinet drawers gaped open.

"Missus Malloy?" She tiptoed in. "Are you all right?"

The CEO, this woman with the power to change the world, who had the personality of a bulldog and the stamina of a thousand men, lifted her head. Her wrinkled skin was saturated with moisture. Tears streamed down her face.

Missus Malloy pushed on the edge of her desk, moving the chair back, and stood. Her tiny stature appeared even more diminutive under the weight of sorrow that had obviously taken over.

"What in the world's the matter?" She stepped up to Missus Malloy, her words soft, intending to comfort. This woman had always had such a prickly personality it had been difficult for Shelley to change her tone in the past, but right now sympathy came from she knew not where.

"I'm so sorry, my dear." Missus Malloy wiped her face with a tissue she'd pulled from a nearby, almost empty Kleenex box.

"For what? What could possibly have you so upset?"

"Much has happened since you left England."

"Oh, dear. Why don't you sit on the sofa and tell me what's wrong. Can I get you some water?" Had John's sweet disposition somehow influenced her own? Never before would she have thought to offer aide to someone at work. Especially not this icon.

Missus Malloy tilted her head, her eyes widening as if to wonder at the change in Shelley's demeanor too. "Why, thank you. A glass of water would be most helpful." Her voice sounded raspy as she dabbed her nose with another tissue, and seemingly tried to restore protocol as the leader of an international company.

After pouring two glasses of sparkling water in crystal stemware, Shelley placed them on the coffee table and sat on the chair opposite Missus Malloy.

They sipped their drinks in silence. The ticking of the large, ornate mantle clock brought Shelley back to days of visiting her grandmother when she'd been a toddler. There had been a small, white wind-up clock in Grandmother's bedroom that had often soothed Shelley's childish fears and lulled her to sleep. The sound in the office seemed to have the same effect as Missus Malloy put down her water and smoothed a stray hair back into place in the otherwise perfect bob.

"There's so much to tell you, I don't know where to start."

Shelley twisted her fingers and bit her lip. This was not going to be good. "I've always found starting at the beginning to be the best place."

John drove up the semi-circle drive. A one-story brick building nestled in trees, idyllic water fountain spurting upward within the pond, trees perfectly trimmed and green lawn ideal for playing croquet was a grand disguise for death within. Lovely as the surrounding grounds were, this place was still preparation for death's welcome, not somewhere to play games or smell flowers in the garden.

He parked, stepped out of the car, closed his eyes and inhaled deeply. It had been quite a while since he'd visited, but it was time to return to where life truly had purpose.

John stepped into the entrance of Heartland Hospice. A beautifully adorned Christmas tree with a nativity scene nested beneath welcomed visitors.

Head Nurse Sue Wallace, starched uniform and broad smile, came from behind the reception and opened her arms wide. "Why, John Cox, how wonderful to see you. It's been some time, hasn't it?" She hugged him with professional bearing, but the sparkle in her eyes was a refreshing dose of love after the recent rejections he'd had from Shelley. How could he have let his emotions toward her get the better of him? It had been a long time since he had found another woman so compelling.

"It's good to be back." He gently squeezed in return.

She stepped back but held his forearms. "Are you here to visit or just popping in to say hello to the staff?"

"I'm actually here to see if you can still use a chaplain? Volunteer basis only for the time being. Although I'm in the process of looking for a new job."

Nurse Sue released him. "Did you discover the real world was a tad bit disappointing after doing such rewarding work here?"

"I thought I could make a difference in the corporate arena, but as Jesus was prone to say, 'It's not the healthy who need a doctor, but the sick.' There are others better qualified to guide and teach God's love to those who think they are healthy. I'm obviously not one of them."

"I'm sure you're giving yourself less credit than you deserve, but that's so like you."

Beep. Beep. Beep.

The all too familiar sound of a monitor announcing a patient in crisis jolted Nurse Sue into action. "I have to go, John. It's so wonderful to see you. Truly. You have much to offer these patients. You know we'd love to have you back." With that she disappeared down the corridor.

There was something to be said about being with others who knew their time had come. A reality about life existed here that those on the outside refused to face. Not prone to being melancholy, John loved sitting with families and talking about the lives they'd experienced with the family member who lay in bed. Joy, sorrow, laughter and pain mixed in harmony like the grand music of the Great Musician who knew each story and every patient who entered this place.

God was here. John was ready to come back home and join Him in His work.

Chapter Twenty-One

SHELLEY WAS USED to bad news. The day her parents were killed replayed in her subconscious. And the prickly sensation that went through her torso and down her arms was a warning sign of impending disaster. She fought the urge to cover her ears as Missus Malloy cleared her throat and took another sip before speaking.

"We noticed something amiss a few months ago. As you might remember, we had that special auditor come and check all the accounts—backwards and forwards, inside and out, leaving no stone unturned. He found something wasn't right."

"I vaguely remember, but I think I had gone on a trip with Patrick to see the Chincoteague ponies when the auditor was here."

"Precisely. You were conveniently away."

"What do you mean?"

"It was an intentional ploy to get you out of the office. Patrick suggested it. To protect you he said."

Shelley bolted upright. "You mean to say you suspected *me* of fraud." She stood and dug one of her long heels into the Persian carpet. "How could you?"

"I'm afraid it wasn't me my dear. Please. Sit down."

Shelley sat back on the edge of the chair ready to bolt if Missus Malloy challenged her integrity again. The two things she believed in above all else were honesty and hard work. Qualities her parents had deeply imbedded in her young life, and ones she'd proudly applied. Her character had never been challenged before, and she wasn't certain how to react. Cry? Get angry? Demand an apology?

"I'm sorry. I knew you weren't involved but there was something awry, and no one could determine the source. The board assumed it was a mistake that would need to be rectified. So we withdrew holdings to cover any discrepancies for the time being. Fully intending to put the funds back in place when possible."

"Whose idea was that? I'm afraid if I'd been asked my opinion, I would have strongly disagreed."

"You would have been spot on." Missus Malloy rose and moved to the window. The setting sun beamed around her small frame giving her silhouette a fiery glow. She moved away from the pane and went behind the desk.

Shelley shifted around in the chair to face her. "And?"

"We left it at that. For a while it seemed the problem was taken care of, but as you know, these things never disappear as easily as we'd like."

"Do you know who's done this? Eventually trails are left behind by every crook."

"It seems our Patrick fooled more than one woman in his life."

"What do you mean?"

"Your precious fiancé, my son..." Missus Malloy took a deep breath as if to stop herself from another round of crying. "He emptied the vaults of Universal Station one slow month at a time into an off-shore account. I'm sad to say, he played us both."

Shelley moved from the chair as if in a trance. "What are you saying?"

"I'm saying he's gone. He's taken everything from us. From you. When he called you to say he was sorry and wanted to go on with the wedding, it was because he knew we were getting close. He was hoping to marry you before he was caught. Then you'd be seen as having colluded with him and would have no choice but to go along with him."

The tightening in Shelley's throat threatened to choke her. She swallowed. "Why would he want to do such a thing?"

Missus Malloy sat back on her desk chair and looked up at Shelley. "I'm to blame I suppose."

"Why would you say that?"

"Because when my husband and I first started this business, it was my brainchild. He was willing to go along for my benefit. But then the company grew bigger than our wildest dreams. It was like a drug, especially for me."

"So why would Patrick turn on you then?"

"Because of all of this." Missus Malloy opened her arms as if to scoop up the office furniture and the glorious trinkets within. "This took me away from what should have mattered most. My husband and son. I didn't realize how Patrick felt and how bitter he was about being second to the company."

"He never mentioned being angry with you." Shelley took the spot by the window and looked over the city. A large swath, resembling the red carpet for Hollywood's finest, spread across the horizon leaving the monuments in the distance like silhouettes against a backdrop.

"Patrick knew you weren't in love with him. But in his own way, I think he loved you and wanted to believe he could make it work. He convinced himself, if he had the money and power, that somehow you would join him in his misdoings."

She turned and leaned on the windowsill. "He had no idea I wouldn't be involved with such despicable behavior. So what happened?"

"Right after he spoke to you, the whole thing blew up in his face. He realized he needed to get away to some place where he couldn't be extradited back to America. Patrick took our private jet to who knows where, and he's the only one who has access to the offshore accounts.

"Right now we're working on freezing those assets. But in the meantime, we've let all the employees except a skeleton crew of drivers and security personnel go. I've let them go with the understanding that if we can get our finances back in order they will be the first to be contacted and offered back their jobs.'

Shelley slumped against the window. "Everything? He took everything?"

"Including the proud Malloy name which I think upsets me the most."

"So what now? Is there anything we can do?"

"I have lawyers working around the clock to sort this out, but it could take months, maybe even years. In the meantime, he's living a life of luxury somewhere south of Mexico presumably." Missus Malloy, elbows on the desk, pressed her face into her palms.

The mantle clock dinged on the quarter hour, and the last sunrays disappeared from view. They sat in graying twilight for what seemed like an eternity, but Shelley glanced at the clock and realized only five minutes had passed. "What can I do to help?"

"I'm afraid there's nothing at this point. It's up to you on whether you want to clear out your office or leave your things in hopes that we can fix this mess."

"But I need to work. This is my life. My dream."

Missus Malloy went to Shelley and guided her gently to the door. "It's been both of our dreams. You're young, full of experience and you can begin again."

"And you?" Shelley stopped at the door.

"Ah. Me. Now that's another matter, isn't it? I have some small holdings I kept from Patrick. Not because I didn't trust him at the time, but I'd forgotten about them in the midst of our expansion."

"Will you be all right? I mean, can I do anything to help you?"

"My dear, what's come over you? I know we haven't seen eye to eye in the past, and I questioned Patrick wanting to marry you. We can both agree that we've had our differences over the years. But you've seemed changed somehow since coming back from London."

Shelley paused, a hand on the doorknob. "I guess spending time with a spiritual advisor had more of an influence than I'd realized."

"Ah, John Cox."

"You sent him with me intentionally, didn't you?" Shelley smiled, but only slightly.

"In the hopes that the two of you would enjoy each other's company and that you would forget Patrick."

"Was it because you…you disliked me so much?"

"Actually, I thought it was for your own benefit. The man's not only attractive, but also brilliant and has the soul of a saint. I love Patrick but I knew you could do better. Even if your goal was to take over the company, John was a much better match for you."

"I'm sorry. Truly sorry." Shelley allowed her exterior shell to crack open a tiny bit. Being vulnerable wasn't as difficult as she had imagined.

"I know, my dear. As we both are."

Shelley left the office and hit the elevator bottom level button. What in the world was she going to do? And how would she survive now that her dreams had been blown away on a wisp of the wind?

The elevator moved rapidly and opened to the emptied foyer. The Universal Station shield hung directly in front with its four quadrants boldly proclaiming the aspirations of an ideal that was now shattered.

Ring. Ring.

Shelley glanced at the phone. The doctor. She'd all but forgotten about him.

Chapter Twenty-Two

AFTER THE DISTRESSING meeting with Missus Malloy, the last thing Shelley wanted to do was answer this call.

She sighed and tapped the phone. "Hello?"

"Shelley Auburn?"

"Yes."

"This is Doctor Bosworth's office. The doctor has asked that you make an appointment to see him as soon as possible."

"I can come first thing tomorrow."

"Does nine o'clock work?"

"That's fine."

"Thank you. We will see you in the morning."

Shelley made her way along the opposite side of the foyer and stepped inside the East Wing elevator. She wanted nothing more than to talk to someone who cared.

Even though she and John had been at odds the last day in England, he had always said he was a reliable friend. Perhaps she'd taken his friendship for granted and treated him unjustly. An apology was in order, but those never came easy.

The noiseless building was akin to walking through a cemetery, and she couldn't shake the prickly sensation of impending doom that had begun in Missus Malloy's office.

Shelley approached John's office, pressed down the few creases on her linen top, and knocked. "John?" She leaned into the door and spoke softer, "It's Shelley. Can we talk? Look. I'm sorry. Really."

With a slight twist of the knob, Shelley entered. Outwardly, the office was the same as it had always been, but somehow the whole aura was different. It was if the peaceful spirit that she always sensed when stepping over the threshold had been dismissed with the rest of the staff. Several items were missing and a stack of boxes leaned against a wall.

Gone was the famous picture of Mister Malloy with his arm draped over John's shoulder in fatherly affection. John had often mentioned how much the picture meant to him. The empty rectangular space on the front of the desk showed where his nameplate had once been. Where could he be? "John?"

"He left a voice message." Missus Malloy was shadowed in the doorframe and stepped into the room. "I just listened to it and came straight over."

"What'd he say?" She already knew the answer. Her racing heart gave voice to the fear pounding in her ears.

"That he wanted to go back to his previous employment and that Universal would do better with a more politically correct spiritual advisor. I wanted to see if I could talk him out of going. We need him more than ever now. But obviously I'm too late."

"This is dreadful." Shelley walked the perimeter of the room and stopped at each photo on the wall, passed the bookshelf and gently caressed the bindings of several books along the way. The heart of the room was gone. "I'm afraid it's my fault. He would've stayed if it hadn't been for me."

"I'm sure that's not true. He seemed to have grown quite fond of you."

"I intentionally let him. I teased, flirted, and egged him on." She stared at Missus Malloy as if just seeing her. "But in the end, I was very unkind."

"They say the hardest lessons in life are the ones we create by our own blind mistakes. It's opening our eyes, learning from them, and changing our behavior that takes courage. John's a good man. I'm sure he'd appreciate hearing what you just said."

"I think my chance of telling him are gone forever. But, yes, he is a good man." She passed Missus Malloy, headed to the locked storage room and retrieved her suitcases. There was nothing more for her here.

Shelley pulled the bedroom drapes aside. Thick morning fog had rolled in, and the white sprinkled covered lawn and shrubs made for ghostly appearances. She spoke to her bedside clock, "I better leave early to give myself plenty of time."

A quick review in the bathroom mirror attested to a rough night sleep that did not bode well with her overall appearance. She tugged gently at baggy eyes. Relaxing under a harsh massage would be just the ticket to get refocused. She would book a place at Michele's Masseuse Parlor later in the day in hopes of temporarily forgetting what had gone on at the office yesterday.

Backing out of the drive, Shelley headed to Doctor Boswell's office. The car's headlights gave little assistance in piercing the thick mist. Oncoming lights appeared like two yellow cat eyes emerging from space. Shelley slowed. Even though the road was as familiar as home, the distorted features of signs and buildings made it difficult to determine her bearings.

Screech.

The din of crushing metal seemed to come after the punch in her gut from the bursting airbag.

Searing pain traveled from her hands, arms and into her chest. Voices shouted, came from nowhere, and surrounded the car. Sirens blared and red strobe lights flashed.

Shelley screamed, and the unrelenting noise outside the car subsided.

"Miss Auburn? Can you hear me?"

Beep, beep, beep. The sound was similar to Shelley's bedroom alarm clock. But who was the woman speaking?

Shelley opened her eyes. This wasn't the familiar room at home. Instead the walls were white and antiseptic smells burned her nostrils.

Throbbing in her right shoulder sent piercing needles along her arm. "What's happened?" She licked dry lips and forced moisture to her raspy throat.

"I'm afraid you were in an automobile accident." A nurse checked the monitor that beeped numbers and rippled waves of electronic signals. "But you're here now, in Saint Andrew's and the doctor will be with you shortly."

"Is it broken?" Raising her right arm was impossible. It seemed a boulder was tied to the fingers on that hand and weighed down the right side of her body.

"Here's the doctor now. He'll explain your situation."

The nurse moved aside and Dr. Gregory House, M.D. stepped up. At least that's who he resembled from the reruns of the medical show "House" she'd seen.

"You've had quite a beating, Miss Auburn. But it could have been much worse. The trauma really came from how the airbag exploded. It saved your life but cracked your clavicle and scapula. Some glass shrapnel from the passenger side window hit your face, but we've stitched it and you should have minimal scarring."

Shelley touched the row of sutures running along her right cheek.

"What's more troublesome are the results of your blood work. Your platelets, and red and white counts are considered borderline."

"That's the irony. I was on my way to the doctor's office about that."

"His name please? We'll call his office and explain why you didn't make your appointment, but I want to also speak to him about these results."

"His name's Doctor Bosworth." What more could possibly go wrong?

"Also, do you have anyone, family or friend, you wish us to contact to come and be with you?"

"No. There's no one."

"I'll be back and check in on you shortly." The nurse tapped Shelley's hand and followed the doctor out.

Shelley choked. Hard as a shell. It was a nickname she'd become accustomed to, and therefore was able to build an emotional wall around. The wall finally breached. Sobbing came from her inner depths and echoed in the empty hospital room. There. Was. No one she could call.

Evening shadows draped the white walls with an ashen tinge. The dim light above the bed was small comfort. Shelley had been used to being alone, but tonight she desperately wanted someone near to hold her, to talk to.

Grandmother had often knelt beside Shelley as a child and recited bedtime prayers. But they seemed ritualistic and without merit. She'd said, "God loves you, little one. Before you go to sleep give your troubles to Him. He'll be up all night anyway. And, remember whenever you feel alone, He's always there."

She had paid little attention. Growing up, the world became the object of her affection and she had been its willing subject. But where had that gotten her?

Should she dare pray? Shelley had treated God as she had so many others, giving Him little attention and never taking Him seriously.

Tears rolled along her cheeks and soaked the pillow. She whispered, "God, I'm so alone. Would You come and keep me company? Please? Grandma said You would."

There was no thunderous cloud or lightning bolt to announce His arrival. "I guess I'm not worthy. How could He ever forgive me?" She turned into the cold, dampened pillow.

Shelley didn't hear an audible voice, but words permeated her inner being as if God spoke directly into her heart. "I *am* with you Shelley Auburn. I always have been. You've just forgotten. Now rest and I'll take care of you."

She closed her eyes and allowed God's peace to wash over her as the monitor's *beep, beep, beep* became a reassuring white-noise that blended with the heartbeat of His forgiveness and love.

Chapter Twenty-Three

SHELLEY MANAGED TO eat most of her breakfast, although the orange Jell-O was a big tricky. After two failed attempts at getting some in a spoon, she gave up.

The television was tuned to reruns of Fixer Upper but merely for company's sake. There was no way she'd be fixing up a home anytime soon. Or moving to Texas, where the show had been filmed.

A nurse entered, checked Shelley's vitals, and proceeded to straighten her pillows and bed linens. She could get used to being spoiled in a hospital if it weren't for the needles, tubes, and agony that went with it.

"Your doctor will be here in approximately ten minutes to give you an update." The nurse twisted the knob to open the window blinds and left.

Shelley muted the television. Did God's intervention last night actually happen? He'd undoubtedly calmed her fears and was the source of a good night's sleep, so she couldn't imagine it being otherwise. Yet doubt still lingered. How could He love and forgive her because of a mere whispered prayer?

"Good morning, Miss Auburn. You look like you're managing quite well." Doctor Davies—a.k.a. *House*—had his nametag on today. He opened a PC and began making medical notes.

"My right side is still sore." She shifted gently upward, managed to pull the top sheet over her stomach and chest, and cringed. "Will I need surgery on my shoulder?"

"Fortunately, the best treatment for this type of fracture is simply a sling. We'll go over how to wear it and what exercises to do in order to keep the area as mobile as possible. What you don't want is the muscles around the scapula to seize up, and the best way to prevent that is proper exercise. Slowly at first, of course."

Shelley laid her head back. "That's a relief. And these stitches?"

"They'll dissolve within a week or so, but I'm afraid there's no guarantee you won't have a bit of a scar. Of course you could've lost an eye, so that's a small price to pay, wouldn't you agree?"

The porcelain skin that she had pampered like a newborn would be forever marred. A constant reminder of the vanity she had flaunted so casually to others. Shelley chewed the tip of her left thumbnail. "Did you speak with Doctor Bosworth?"

"Yes. Turns out we were colleagues at Vanderbilt. He's asked to come and see you when he makes his own rounds later on. If you feel up to it, of course. Otherwise, you can rest here for the next twenty-four hours or so, and when you get home you can make an appointment with his office."

"If I'm going to be sitting here, I might as well get the whole ordeal over with. Please ask him to come."

"Certainly. Now, do you have any other questions?"

"I don't think so."

"Needless to say, you won't be able to drive until most of the healing occurs and that won't be for several weeks. Are you sure there isn't anyone we can contact to help you? Or assist you in getting home."

"I'm afraid not, but I'll manage. A taxi can pick me up, and I have an elderly neighbor who will probably be willing to check in with me periodically. I've taken care of her cat quite often. I'm sure she won't mind."

"I'll leave you to rest, and I'll be back later in the day." He closed the PC. "Try and get some sleep. The medicine should help."

She slid down and lowered the bed to a prone position.

Knock. Knock.

Shelley moaned. The drugs had had the desired effect. "Who's there?" she muttered, and focused on the pinpoint of light coming from the partially opened door.

"May I come in?" Without permission to do so, Doctor Bosworth entered her room.

"Sure. Be my guest." The numbness in her tongue made the words slur.

"I see they have you sedated. How are you feeling?"

"I've had better days."

Doctor Bosworth reviewed some handheld notes, as Shelley managed to keep one eye open and observe him.

"My, you did have a nasty accident."

"I understand it could've been worse."

"We might want to wait until you're feeling better." He moved to the monitor.

She shook her head. "No. Please. Tell me. We've put this off long enough."

"As we've discussed, your blood count has been quite low." The doctor's tone was somber as if he were a mortician speaking to the family of the deceased.

"Go on." Fighting the effects of the medicine, she scooted up on her left elbow and moaned.

"Please don't move. You'll only injure yourself further. The best thing you can do right now is heal. You've got a long road ahead of you."

"You aren't just talking about the road to recovery from this mishap, are you?"

"I'm afraid not. Quite honestly I've been surprised you've gone this long without fainting spells or falls."

"Oh, dear."

"What?"

"I did faint while in England, but I put it down to stress."

Doctor Bosworth slid the oversized blue plastic chair from the corner closer to the bedside. He sat, bowed his head, and put his hands into a pyramid as if to pray. "You, my dear, are a sick young lady."

Icy fingers of death gripped Shelley. The impending doom from yesterday's devastating news resurfaced. She shivered, and the doctor stood, tightened the blanket around her legs and thighs, and sat back down.

His eyes clouded as he wiped his forehead. Doctor Bosworth took her left hand and his warm touch helped the shaking to subside.

"Is it...is it...terminal?" What a calculating word. Terminal. Finale. A finish line in view of ones's life race.

"There's hope, Miss Auburn. The success rate with these types of illnesses has skyrocketed with recent medical discoveries. You're young and healthy. I have great hopes for your future."

"But?"

"But it won't be easy. I won't sugarcoat the process you'll go through in the next several months."

She squeezed his hand. "What is it exactly?"

"The medical term is Aplastic Anemia. Aplastic is the inability of stem cells to generate mature blood cells and affects the bone marrow's reproduction."

"That sounds like a laptop whose hard drive has a major virus."

"Precisely."

"How do we erase this virus from my computer?" Somehow referring to this situation in terms of machines and megabytes made it more antiseptic and less personal. If she could just keep it at arms distance, perhaps the reality of the situation wouldn't be as difficult.

"There are several options, and I can refer you to a specialty hospital such as M.D. Anderson if you prefer a second opinion. However, chemotherapy and bone marrow transplants are prescribed. For the moment, you need to heal from this accident. You must be as healthy as possible for us to move forward."

"I understand."

"I'm sorry to bring more bad news after you've had such a trauma." Doctor Bosworth stood.

"Thank you for taking the time to come and see me. I'm not sure what to say or do next."

"I say go to sleep. Wake up and begin healing. We'll come up with a solution to eradicate this worm from your internal drive." He chuckled gently. "I promise to do everything in my ability to make that happen." Doctor Bosworth touched her knee, offered a slight smile and left the room.

The coldness seeped into her muscles and tightened like a rubber band stretched too tight and would certainly snap.

"God. Help me. Please. Everything I've relied on—my looks, a future with a company I've slaved for, my body—are worthless. How did this happen? What can I do?" Tears rolled down her temples into the pillow and saturated her hair.

She had more questions than answers. She had missed out on so much in life that was important because all she'd thought about was how important she was. Now what mattered most was discovering what she needed to do with the rest of the life God had ordained for her.

Chapter Twenty-Four

THE HOSPITAL QUIETED as visiting hours ended and evening preparations took place. A turnover in staff would occur soon, medicines would be distributed and window shades drawn.

Shelley could no more go to sleep than she could eat the food they had put in front of her for dinner. Her life had turned upside down. But the outside world would move on regardless of what happened. People would still marry and others have babies. Hospital beds would clear one patient while other patients waited to take their place. It was the cycle of life.

The ambulance staff at the scene of the accident had managed to collect several of Shelley's personal items, including her leather briefcase. She had thrown it in the car at the last minute in order to start writing a resume while waiting at the doctor's office.

She reached for the bedside cord and rang the nurse's desk.

"What can I do for you?" The young chirpy, bright-eyed evening nurse named Kelly danced in.

"Would you mind getting my laptop, please?" She nodded toward the wardrobe where they'd placed her belongings.

"Why, certainly." Nurse Kelly practically skipped to the cupboard and pulled out Shelley's case. "Is there anything else I can do for you?"

"No, thank you."

"If you need anything else, please ring the bell." Out the door the nurse bounced with Tigger-like enthusiasm.

Shelley closed her eyes momentarily. "Lord, how do others cope with being told they have cancer?" She opened the laptop and typed in the password with one-handed awkwardness. Where could she possibly find out about how to deal with what lay ahead?

"Miss Auburn?" A smartly dressed woman in high heels and classic navy suit entered. "I'm Miss Godfrey. I know it's past visiting hours but I thought I'd pop in for a few minutes and give you some material before I leave for the night."

The woman's perfect translucent skin caused Shelley to cup her right cheek. Her face would never be the same. Her hand slid off her cheek, and gently closed her laptop. Somehow that no longer mattered. "What can I do for you, Miss Godfrey?"

"I work in the hospital as a patient representative. Doctor Bosworth stopped in my office this afternoon. He asked that I come by and give you some brochures and my number." She placed a packet on the side table and pulled out a single sheet. "I help patients diagnosed with cancer find local support groups. It's imperative that they—that you—have others to talk with during this time. It's a means of encouraging one another."

"Thank you," Shelley barely whispered. Cancer. How did one speak that word and not cringe with horror? She cleared her throat. "Maybe you're an answer to my prayer? I was just looking online to see what I could find out."

Miss Godfrey cheeks flashed pink. "How kind. It's not every day I'm told I'm an answer to prayer. May I give you a word of caution, though?"

"Of course." Shelley liked this woman. Not only was she professional, she was pleasant.

"Be very careful how you use the Internet to find information. It's a blessing and a curse. There are several websites in this packet that we recommend patients use. Otherwise you're likely to get bogged down in ones with the absolute worse-case scenarios and probably the most unreliable information. It can play with your mind, believe me."

"That's good advice."

"As I was saying, there are support groups in the area and I can recommend this particular one that meets every third Thursday of the month. Of course, that's two nights from today so you may not be up to it yet." Miss Godfrey offered her the slip of paper.

"I guess I'll see how I'm feeling, but the sooner I get to grips with what's ahead the better I'll be."

"The woman in charge of the meeting, Francine Carmichael, has her phone number and email address on that form. Be sure to contact her. I'm sure she'd be happy to help you in any way. She's a personal friend of mine, and a cancer survivor herself. You two will get along wonderfully, I'm sure."

"Thank you." Shelley choked. "I mean that. You're the first person I've spoken to about this. Does it get easier?"

Miss Godfrey's tender smile and sparkling eyes told Shelley that somehow this woman understood. "I believe so. Because the more you speak with others that have gone through this same situation, the more hope you have. At least that's what my friend Francine has told me. It's the reason she started this group."

"Thank you again."

"It's my pleasure, Miss Auburn. If you ever need me or ever just want to talk, please feel free to call my cell anytime. My number is in the packet."

"You aren't doing this just because it's in your job description, are you? You seem to like what you do."

"I love it. I offered you my cell phone because I want to help, not because it's required." Miss Godfrey took Shelley's hand. "I'll leave now so you can get some sleep. But, please contact Francine. She'd loved to help you, too."

"I will."

Shelley turned off the light, and clicked on the television again, making sure the volume was down low. Sleep would be elusive, but the tiniest flicker of hope burned within.

A taxi waited curbside as Shelley was pushed on a wheelchair to its door. Last night's sleep was aided by medicine and moving into morning's bright daylight stirred a modicum of energy. With God's help she'd make it. Somehow.

It was a ten-minute drive to her apartment. The cab driver helped her up the stairs and her neighbor waited by Shelley's front door. She'd sent a quick text to let her neighbor know about her accident.

"I wasn't expecting to see you." Shelley smiled and cringed with pain at the same time.

"I've brought you some soup."

"Thank you. How very thoughtful."

"I'll be here every morning and night to check on you. You've always been kind enough to watch my precious Kitty when I've been gone, it's the least I can do."

Shelley never realized how the smallest efforts of kindness could reap the greatest rewards.

"Be sure to call me if you need anything." The woman's silver hair sparkled in the kitchen's overhead light as she placed the pot on the stove. "I've missed having someone to take care of. I nursed my Peter until, well, until he went to heaven."

"I'm sorry."

"I miss him terribly at times." She turned to Shelley, eyes damp from tears, but her wrinkled mouth held a smile. "Somehow, I think you and I are going to start a great friendship, aren't we?"

"Oh, I hope so." Shelley shuffled to a chair and sat. "I'm a bit weak though. I think I'll go and lie down for a little while. But if you're around and want to come over this afternoon, I'd love your company."

"I'll see you then." The door closed and quietness settled in.

"Thank you, Lord." Shelley had missed so many gifts each day had offered as she flew from one meeting to another, trying to reach the top of the corporate ladder. No more. The doctors, Miss Godfrey and her neighbor were presents she would not take for granted. They were definitely better than anything a glass-ceilinged office had to give.

John pedaled his bicycle up the steep incline. He had chosen this route intentionally, to get the best workout possible and enough energy burned to sear away Shelley's image that haunted his every waking hour. Even sleep had been disrupted since he packed his things and left Universal.

He pumped harder and finally reached the pinnacle. The city was magnificent. There was no doubt this country should be proud of its Capital, the center of American dreams. Where the poor, downtrodden, and underprivileged could hope for a better tomorrow.

Shelley had a dream that he never understood. Her drive to be in charge of the largest corporation of the computer world was beyond him. She had so much to offer others. He just knew it. He shook his head. It seemed the horrendous climb up the hill did little to eradicate her from his mind.

John turned around and headed back down the road. Heartland Hospice had asked him to participate in the cancer rehabilitation group held in the conference room tonight. Although Heartland wasn't usually the venue for these people, their normal meeting place was undergoing renovation and they'd ask for a room this one time.

Heartland needed a staff member to be present during the course of the meeting. He was accustomed to speaking one on one to patients facing death. This would be a new experience for him. One he wasn't particularly looking forward to.

Chapter Twenty-Five

SHELLEY STRETCHED HER good arm and gently rotated the other. It would take time. But after another good night's sleep and plenty of wonderful food from her neighbor she was ready to meet Francine and the others in the cancer support group that evening.

After several emails passed between Shelley and Francine, she had the necessary details. The address had been changed from their regular location and they would meet at 1127 Woodstone Drive at seven-thirty.

The taxi driver knew the location, and she arrived a few minutes before the meeting was due to begin.

Five women and two men sat around an oval conference table. Idyllic scenes of white sand beaches and seaside towns in ornate frames adorned the walls while Christmas music played softly in the background. Holidays had never been her thing since her parents were gone. Now the reality of what Christmas meant became clear. The reason for the season was indeed Jesus, God's own Son. She closed her eyes for a brief moment to listen to Silent Night before entering the room to find an empty seat.

"Everyone, please welcome Shelley Auburn," Francine said,

as Shelley pulled out the chair closest to the door. The others nodded and smiled broadly.

Her heart fluttered like a trapped butterfly. She'd always been the one in charge, expecting that others would just jump onboard as she commandeered the gathering.

"Miss Auburn, would you mind closing the door behind you? We won't disturb the residents that way. Oh, please dim the lights as well. It'll be easier to see the slides."

"Sure." She closed the gray metallic door with a long rectangular beveled glass, lowered the lights and sat.

As the power point presentation began, a rap on the door stopped Francine mid-sentence. "Please excuse me for a moment."

Francine exited and was back within seconds. "Miss Auburn, it seems someone would like to speak to you."

"Me?"

"Yes. Says he needs to ask you a few questions."

"How strange." Shelley grabbed her purse.

"We'll wait for you to return before we begin." Francine turned the lights back up. "We can have a few minutes of discussion first. That way you won't miss the pertinent information."

"That's very kind." Kindness was a new concept. So unlike how Shelley had treated others who attended her briefings. But the superiority and frozen barricade she'd built around her over the years had begun to thaw as others had shown such loving care these past few days.

She stepped outside. His back turned to her, a tall gentleman with broad shoulders and dark hair seemed familiar. She shook her head. Would she forever see John in others and ache the loss?

The man turned.

She inhaled. "John?" Could it really be him? A staff badge was clipped to his shirt, and that wonderful curl drooped over his forehead. Shelley held her cheek momentarily. Her stitches burned from saturating tears.

She walked in his direction, slowly, as if in a dream.

"It's true. It is *you*. I read your name on the list of attendees." He glanced at his iPhone. "I thought it must be some mistake." John moved one short step toward her.

Shelley stopped and whispered, "I thought I'd never see you again."

"But why are you here?"

She moved another step nearer yet remained an arm's length away. She wanted to throw herself into his arms like a human cannonball, but her impulsiveness had gotten her in trouble with him in the past. Now was not the time. "I've much to tell you. But the first thing I want to say is, I'm so very, very sorry."

He stepped closer. "For what? You always said you were never one to apologize. You didn't see the necessity."

His nasal voice sounded as if he'd been crying. "You're right. How vain I've been. Believe me though when I say I never meant to hurt you. All I want to ask is, if you can find in it in your heart to forgive me." She moved a half-inch closer.

"There's nothing to forgive. You have your goals, and I won't stand in the way."

"But that's the thing...my goals, those aspirations I clawed my way to achieve have...well, they're...they're just not important anymore."

"Why the change? What's happened?"

"Guess you could say I've learned some lessons the hard way." She held up her sling-encased arm at a low angle.

"What did you do?" He nodded toward her arm.

"I was in an automobile accident."

"What? Are you all right?" John stepped closer.

"I'll recover."

"That's not all that's happened since I saw you last, is it?

You seem different. Softer. There's a gentleness I'm not sure I've seen before."

Shelley moved into John's personal space. She knew her heart would forever belong to him. But would he run? Had she injured this man one too many times? "The company's gone, my career's over, and I'm getting ready to face something dreadful." She barely whispered her last few words. "I just can't imagine going through it alone."

"You're not alone, Shelley. I'm here for you. I've *always* been here for you."

Shelley asked, "But why are *you* here? Is this your new job?"

"Yes and no. I used to work here. That's when I met Kathy. She was a patient, and in a short amount of time we fell in love."

"I never knew. How terribly selfish I've been not asking about your life."

"My time with her was short, but she changed me forever. When she died, I left here and went to Universal. I needed to get away. But now I know this is where I belong. Where I've always belonged."

"I'm so sorry for your pain, your loss."

"It's all right."

Shelley whispered and cupped his cheek, "I need you, John.".

"And I need you."

"I'm so glad God brought you into my life." His eyes. Those eyes that had laughed, been angry with her, and had held her attention like no other. They pooled with tears and he drew her gently in with his arm around her waist, their breath mixing. She reached up, put the drooping curl back in its place and welcomed his passionate kiss.

They separated slightly, but John still held her firmly. "Let's go back into the meeting together? With God's help, we can get through whatever the future holds. From now on we'll make plans together, shall we?"

Shelley nodded. "We shall."

The conference door closed behind them as the others welcomed them into the room. What the future held was anyone's guess. Shelley squeezed John's arm as he pulled out a chair for her and sat. This would indeed be a never-forgotten Christmas, no matter what the future held.

The overhead lights dimmed, and the power point presentation began as their hands intertwined and Shelley found herself finally at peace with the man she loved.

Other books by Beatrice Fishback

Fiction:
Murder in the Air
Winter Writerland
Summer of the Missing Muse
Spring Scribe
Autumn Author
Bethel Manor
Bethel Manor Reborn
Bethel Manor Secrets
Dying to Eat at the Pub
Loving a Selfie
Christmas at the Corp
Christmas Prodigal

Non-fiction:
Loving Your Military Man
Defending the Military Marriage
Defending the Military Family

www.beasattitudes.net

Made in the USA
Columbia, SC
14 April 2023